DANNY ORLIS
and the
CANADIAN CAPER

DANNY ORLIS
and the
CANADIAN CAPER

by

BERNARD PALMER

MOODY PRESS

CHICAGO

© 1972 by
THE MOODY BIBLE INSTITUTE
OF CHICAGO

ISBN: 0-8024-7237-0

Printed in the United States of America

Contents

1

Barney Presents a Problem

DEL DAVIS was glad the football season at Fairview, Minnesota, was almost over. It gave him an opportunity to go out in the woods around the Orlis home again to get reacquainted with his pets. He never tired of them.

His deer, Jumper, was still around; although he seldom came up into the yard anymore. Del saw him out in the woods now and again. The beautiful buck would stand quite still, eyeing him questioningly, as though he almost remembered him. At times, he would allow Del to approach within a dozen feet before he whirled to race away.

Del didn't mind that. He was glad to see that Jumper was afraid of people again. It would help the charming creature to avoid the guns and arrows of the hunters that surged through the Minnesota forests every November.

Blackie, Del's pet crow, was always around the place, regardless of the season. He no longer thought about going South for the winter, like his self-respecting brothers and sisters did. He was happy enough on the Orlis farm with the Davis triplets. When he was bored or lonely, he would perch saucily on the clothesline, screaming for attention. "Play ball, Del! Play ball! Run, Doug, run!"

In cold weather, the lanky boy left a small window open in the barn, so his ebony pet could go in, out of the wind and snow. Blackie was grateful in his arrogant, disrespectful way. As soon as Del stepped outside, the crow would come swooping down at him and light on his shoulder.

Doug Davis had scoffed at his triplet's love for animals and birds before; but now that the tension was gone between them and they were truly brothers once more, he found that he enjoyed being with Del and his animal friends. He was surprised that Del had learned so much about the animals and birds in their area.

He could recognize most of the birds by sight and many of them by their calls. He knew the scientific names of the snowbirds, the sparrows, and the others who wintered there. He knew the habits of the animals, the kinds of nests or homes they fixed, what they ate, and where he would be apt to find them. And what he didn't know, he would ask Barney. Usually, the elderly Cree Indian could tell him.

Doug enjoyed the weekly visits to the Indian's little cabin almost as much as Del did. At times Barney would be in a mood to tell stories about his younger days, when he was strong and sharp of eye; and game roamed the Saskatchewan forests in abundance. There were still large numbers of moose and deer around the Indian's former home, but the wolverine were gone and now the trappers had difficulty in getting good catches of wild mink and otter and lynx.

The old Indian seemed to have the capacity to remember most of what had happened to him and was able to relate it in vivid detail. He told about the bears he had tangled with on his trapline in northern Saskatchewan, and laughed with Del and Doug until tears cleaned a furrow on either cheek, as he told them about the wolverine that had gotten into his cabin and the trouble the animal had caused.

As Barney talked, it seemed to the boys that he was transported into the frozen North, where he could feel the bite of the subzero wind and hear the snow crunch under foot. Just listening, they knew the pain of the icy blast that tingled his cheeks and frosted his breath.

The boys hoped they would be able to remember all the stories Barney told about the far North. They had never heard anything half so captivating. But Barney talked about more than his experiences hunting and trapping, when they visited him. Whenever he could, he turned the conversation to the things of Christ. He talked about the days before he became a Christian; how he was a slave to sin, and how later he talked with his people about his God.

"And you know what I told them?" he went on. "I said, when I want to talk to God, I don't have to make a sacrifice to the spirits. I don't have to put any cloth in the bush or burn sweet grass and tobacco to make God come so I can talk to Him. I go out under a spruce tree and get down on my knees, and I say, 'God, this is old Barney. I used to believe all those things some of my people still believe, but not anymore. I'm going to walk Your way now, and when I die, I know that You're going to take me up to heaven.' "

Del and Doug listened, transfixed, while the elderly Indian continued.

"When I was younger and could work a big trapline, I used to make a lot of money. Sometimes I'd have five or six hundred dollars in my pocket. But I never was happy, or satisfied, either. There was always something wrong, something to make me uneasy. But now—" A grin teased the corners of his mouth and sparked his dark eyes. "But now I'm always happy. I guess I'm like Paul. Now that I'm a Christian, it doesn't make any difference whether I have any money or whether my pockets are full or empty. I'm as happy as can be."

Del hitched his chair closer to the table. "I wish I could feel the same way," he murmured. "I wish I could love God so much that I'd be happy no matter what happens to me."

"You *can* feel the same way." A new tenderness crept into his voice. "All you must do is turn your whole life over to Jesus, and let Him do what He wants to with you."

At other times, Barney would open the Bible and have one of the boys read it to him, or they would memorize verses together. They hadn't known that could be so much fun. And, what pleased both of them the most was that they felt a greater closeness to God, being with Barney.

But Barney wasn't always exuberant. On one occasion late that fall, he was quiet and pensive. Del and Doug were disturbed by his mood.

"What's the matter, Barney?" Del asked. "Is there something wrong?"

At first, the old Indian tried to brush the question aside. "Now, what could be wrong with me?" he asked jovially.

"Don't you feel good?" Doug broke in. He knew that Barney had heart trouble.

Barney sighed deeply and tugged at the lobe of his ear with nervous fingers. "I feel all right, I guess. Only—"

Doug broke in. "Only what?"

"I just get lonesome to see my family, that's all."

"If that's all it is," Del said, "why don't you go and see them? That wouldn't take so long, especially if you flew."

"I know that; but if a fella doesn't have any money, he's not going to be able to go anywhere these days." Then he added quietly, "and that's the fix I'm in. I don't have any money for a ticket."

On the way home, Del turned to his brother and said, "I feel so sorry for Barney, I can hardly stand it. There ought to be *some* way we can fly him up to Canada to see his family."

"Sure there is. All we have to do is buy him a ticket."

Del beamed. "Do you suppose we could?"

Doug faced him, his lower jaw sagging. "Are you serious?"

"I don't know of any better use for money right now, do you?"

"No," Doug said thoughtfuly. "Only we're both in about the same fix old Barney is. We don't have anything, either."

What Doug said was true. They didn't have any money and little chance of getting any. They didn't even have jobs.

"Maybe we could find work somewhere," Del said.

"I wish we could." A pensive, wistful tone crept into Doug's voice. "I sure wish we could."

The boys prayed about Barney's problem for the next few days, asking God to help them find a way to earn the money the elderly Cree needed. Although they didn't say anything to anyone else about their concern, Danny sensed a change in their manner.

"What's the matter with you guys?"

DeeDee glanced impishly at them. "Maybe they're in love."

Doug made a face at her. "That's all you can think about."

"That's right," Del put in. "We're not like you. We have something else on our minds."

"Like what?" she prodded.

They hesitated.

"What's the matter?" Danny asked. "Is it something you can't tell us?"

Doug shook his head. "It isn't that. It's just that we had decided we wouldn't say anything to anyone about it. But I guess it'd be all right, don't you think?" he asked Del. So they related Barney's problem.

"Isn't there *anything* we can do?" DeeDee asked tenderly.

"That's what we've been trying to decide. Like Doug says, it wouldn't be so hard if we had the money to buy him a ticket."

"Couldn't we go out and talk to people and ask them to give money to help buy the ticket?" she asked. "I wouldn't mind going to some of the people in our church. I just *know* lots of them would give for Barney. Everybody who knows him, loves him."

"Oh, no," Del broke in quickly. "Barney wouldn't like that. He wouldn't want to think that people were treating him as a charity case."

"You were talking about *us* raising the money for him to make the trip," she countered.

"But that's different. Barney is so close to us he's—he's practically family."

2

Into the Wild Blue Yonder

A MONTH WENT BY, and Doug and Del prayed a lot about Barney and the money needed for him to go back to Canada to visit his children. When they couldn't find regular after school work, they tried to line up odd jobs to earn a few dollars. They managed to get a number of jobs shoveling snow, and one of the women in the church paid them to help clean out her basement. But the money was slow coming in, when they compared what they had with what they needed.

"I don't think we're *ever* going to have enough," Doug said as they hurried home over the snow-packed road.

"Maybe we can do better, now that Christmas vacation's almost here."

"Do you know how much we still need to buy his ticket? Over a hundred dollars." Doug kicked a piece of ice along the road. "There's just no way that you and I are going to be able to earn enough money to fly Barney to his home and back. Let's face it."

Del's frown spread across his lean face. He didn't like to admit that they were defeated, but he agreed with Doug. There didn't seem to be any way they could raise the money for Barney's trip, even if they could work all through vacation, which wasn't likely. Most guys had their jobs lined up weeks ahead of time.

"Maybe DeeDee had the best idea after all."

Del shook his head. "No way. Barney wouldn't take charity from the church people, you know that. It might even make him feel bad if we tried it."

Doug's shoulders shrugged. "I suppose you're right, but I can't stand to think of him having to stay at home because we aren't able to find jobs to earn the money for his ticket."

"Me too."

When the boys reached home, Danny Orlis was waiting for them. "And where've you guys been?" he demanded in mock severity.

"Trying to find something to do to help us to earn a little money."

Doug peeled off his heavy coat and hung it in the closet. "But we didn't find a thing."

Del said, "To tell you the truth, it's been a bust. We don't even have twenty-five dollars yet."

"And how far could he get on that amount?" Doug added, showing his discouragement.

A grin teased the corners of Danny's mouth. "It just might go a little further than you think."

They stared at him questioningly. "What do you mean?"

"Yeh," Del added. "Where's he going to buy a ticket to northern Saskatchewan for twenty-five dollars?"

"Maybe he won't need a ticket. What do you think of that?"

For the first time, the boys saw the excitement that he was trying to hide.

"What's the deal, Danny?"

"I don't know whether I ought to tell you or not," he teased.

Del faced Kay. "What is it, Kay? What's he talking about?"

"It's Danny's secret. I wouldn't dare give it away."

"Barney won't take charity, or did you know that?" Del informed him.

"Who said anything about charity?"

The boys scooted forward on their chairs and leaned toward Danny intently. At last he relented. "OK, I'll tell you. But I really shouldn't. I ought to let you stew for a few more days. You're doing a lot of work, building up your muscl—"

"What *is* it?" Del broke in.

"The mission wants me to fly up to northern Saskatchewan next Monday, so I'll be able to take Barney to his home on the way and pick him up on the way back two weeks later."

"Man!" Doug exclaimed. "That's great!"

"I'll say it is!"

"And, Kay and I have been talking about something else. We just might be able to squeeze you two into the aircraft and take you along."

Del and Doug stared at him.

"You're kidding!"

"Well, if you don't want to go—"

"We didn't say that!" they chorused. "That'll be terrific!"

Danny and the boys left the house while it was still dark that Monday morning and stopped at Barney's cabin for him. When they got there, he was standing in the middle of the floor, his overcoat and cap already on and his suitcase by the door.

His eyes lighted when he saw Del and Doug. "Well now, I'm real glad you two are going with me," he said. "It's going to make the trip all the better."

Del took his suitcase and carried it out to the car. "I think we're a lot more excited about going than you are to have us along. It's going to be great visiting your village and getting acquainted with that grandson of yours."

Barney climbed into the front seat with Danny, while the boys pushed into the back seat. It was a minute or more before he spoke. Just lifting himself into the car seemed to make Barney huff and puff.

"There's one thing I forgot to tell you about my grandson George," he began, his face looking uncharacteristically serious. "He isn't a Christian. I've talked and talked to him about God, but he doesn't seem to want to understand."

"I've met a few guys like that myself," Danny said.

Barney's smile flashed again. "Maybe God is letting Del and Doug go with me so they can show George that it's possible to give your life to Jesus Christ and still be a real man."

"I don't know that we would be very good examples for him," Del said uneasily. "I sure don't feel like much of an example."

Danny flew to Regina, where they landed to clear customs and to refuel. At first he debated whether to spend the night in the Saskatchewan provincial capital, but finally decided that there was still enough daylight left to go on.

The next stop was the little village beyond the roads where Barney's family lived. Danny located the runway they had cleared on the frozen lake, circled the village, and landed. At the first sound of the engine, men and boys appeared from the houses and began to make their way to the landing strip. The women came too, but they weren't as brave as the men, and stayed some distance behind.

Danny glanced in Barney's direction as he made his approach. "It looks as though you're going to have a little welcoming committee."

"Yeh," Del said, "like everybody in the village."

"Do people always come out like this when you land in one of these villages, Danny?" Doug wanted to know.

"Most of the time we attract quite a crowd when we land at a village up here. It isn't often some of these places see a strange plane, and everyone wants to know who's come and why."

"I'll bet they'll be happy this afternoon." Del glanced at Barney, who was trying hard to keep the excitement from showing on his broad face.

Expertly Danny Orlis brought the skis down to the ice without a bump and taxied to a halt. Someone in the crowd recognized Barney, as Danny shut off the engine, and a number of people separated themselves from the others and surged forward to greet the elderly Indian.

Barney's lips trembled slightly as he went from one to another, grasping an outstretched hand, squeezing another man's arm with his gnarled fingers, and enveloping two tiny girls in his huge bear hug. They squealed with delight and chattered to him in Cree.

Del and Doug Davis were grinning broadly. "They must be two of his granddaughters," Del suggested.

"Yeh, he told me they're George's younger sisters," Doug explained.

After a time Barney disengaged himself from his relatives and old friends and introduced Danny and the boys to them.

"And this is my grandson George," he said at last.

George Aubichon smiled shyly. He spoke to Doug and Del, but said no more, for the moment. He would have to get better acquainted first to find out if they liked him before he would open up and be friendly.

It was seldom that a strange aircraft landed at their village. That in itself was an occurrence of some note. But to have youthful visitors get off! George could not remember ever having seen anyone his own age come in to visit.

Barney had already planned that Doug and Del would stay with George at his son's, so they would have someone their own age to hang around with. He planned to visit his only daughter first. Danny, who was only staying the night, could go to the home of Barney's younger brother.

That was agreeable with the missionary pilot. He knew the houses in the little Cree village were small, and there wouldn't be room for all of them at the same place. He knew, too, that he would be welcomed wherever he stayed.

George Aubichon was shy, but he was also very pleased when his grandfather told him that Del and Doug would be staying with him. Pride shone on his face, as he led his guests past the knot of envious fellows his own age. He would let them all get acquainted with his new friends before they had to leave, but right now he was going to keep them for himself.

Doug and Del didn't know that George had already accepted them, and for a time they were afraid the slight, dark-eyed lad would never let them get acquainted with him. But after an hour or so, he talked as much as any of their friends.

"It's a good thing for us your school's out for a few days, George," Doug told him. "You can show us this part of Canada."

"It wouldn't make any difference to me if school was out or not," he retorted, only the slightest trace of accent marring his English. "I'd take off and show you around, anyway."

"That might not be so good when the time comes

for you to get your grades. Back home they take off our grade average if we miss a lot of school," Del told him.

George shrugged. "Who cares? I'm goin' to quit school after this year anyway."

They stared at him. They were used to hearing guys talk about not liking school and wanting to quit; there were times when they said the same sort of thing themselves. But even when they did, they knew that they didn't mean it. It was different with George. There was a tone of finality in his voice.

"I can go to high school if I want to, and the government will pay for it," he said. "Any of the kids can. But I'll let my sister, Alice, do the studying for our family. She's good with books. She can go to school in my place."

"That won't do you much good."

George changed the subject abruptly, as though to show them that school didn't mean much to him one way or the other. "What I *really* like to do," he continued, "is trap. Have you guys ever worked a trapline?"

Doug spoke for both of them. "We've done a little trapping. I guess we've set out traps almost every year we've lived on the farm."

"Yeh," Del said, "but we've never caught very much. All we catch out our way are a few 'rats and squirrels, or maybe a skunk."

"Your granddad has shown us all we know about trapping, but that's not very much," Doug went on. "We don't know much about making good sets. I guess that's our biggest trouble."

George drew himself erect, proudly. There was one thing he did know a lot about, he told himself; that was trapping. Few of the guys his age in the village were able to trap half as well as he did. "I do real good with my traps," he said. He wasn't boasting, just stating a fact. "I've already trapped six beaver and four mink and twenty-seven squirrels this year."

They were sauntering along the path in the direction of the Hudson Bay trading post as they talked. George's home was nearby. It was beginning to snow again, fine, powdery flakes almost like flour, sifting through the still, subzero air.

"Only now it is not so good," he added softly.

Del eyed him curiously. "What's the matter?" he asked. There was a strange, mysterious quality in the way the Indian boy spoke.

"It isn't that I've lost my luck," George went on. "I still catch plenty of furs in my traps." He stopped and turned to face them, speaking in a taut whisper. "But somebody is stealing them. They work my traps before I get to them."

Del Davis could still picture the little village as

they had circled it before landing. Surely people who lived so close together in such a vast wilderness would not steal from one another.

"You must be mistaken about someone stealing your pelts," he told the Indian boy.

George pulled in a thin breath and expelled it thoughtfully. "All I know is that I caught two beaver last week, but didn't get either skin. Somebody took them out of the traps. Only a few hairs and some blood were left."

The boys thought about that momentarily. "Could it be someone from outside your village?"

George shrugged. "Who knows?" Then, new hope flickered in his eyes. "You'll be here for a week. You can help me catch him, eh?"

Doug gasped and looked questioningly at his brother. They had only figured on visiting in the village for a few days, until Danny came back to pick them up. They hadn't figured on getting in on anything like this.

George repeated his question. "Will you help me?"

"We'll do what we can." Del spoke reluctantly, as though he would rather not have any part of it, but couldn't quite figure how to turn George down.

The Indian boy's grin was warm and contagious. "We'll go out on the trapline tomorrow and catch whoever it is who's stealing my skins. Then he'll be sorry."

Doug muttered under his breath to Del, "I just hope we're not the ones who'll be sorry."

3

To Catch a Thief

DEL AND DOUG lay awake in their little bedroom for a long while that night, whispering tensely to each other. It would have been hard to tell which one was more disturbed about George and his request for help. And the worst of it was, there was no way of backing out.

"I sure didn't think we were going to get in on anything like this when we came up here," Doug said, almost putting his mouth in Del's ear so he wouldn't be overheard. "Did you?"

His brother shivered. "To tell you the truth, it gives me the creeps just to think about it. It's hard enough to catch a fur thief, but you know something? He'll have a gun."

"How do you know that?"

"Almost every trapper carries some kind of a gun to kill the animals in his traps."

Doug swallowed against the lump in his throat. "I'm beginning to think we'd be smart to go back to Fairview where we belong."

"And just exactly how are we going to do that?"

"I wish I knew."

Del rolled over on his back and stared up at the ceiling in the blackness of the night. "We could back out," he murmured. He waited hopefully.

"And have George think we're too scared to help him?" Doug replied.

"It'd be the truth, wouldn't it?"

Silence hung like a curtain between them. "George thinks as much of his neck as we do ours. He's not going to let us in on anything that's too dangerous," said Doug optimistically.

"Only, his idea and ours about what's too dangerous may not be the same. Did you ever think of that?" Del showed his nervousness by snapping at his brother.

"I guess you're right, but I'd still like to try to help him. We can always back out, if we think someone is apt to get hurt."

Del still wasn't anxious to be involved in the trapline mystery, but he could see that his brother was growing more excited all the time. "Let's knock it off and go to sleep," he murmured. "We don't have to decide anything tonight."

When the Davis boys got up the next morning,

the conversation of the night before seemed to be a vague, unrealistic dream. George's mother was padding soundlessly about the kitchen in her mukluks when they came out, making porridge and tea for their breakfast.

Del went to the window and looked out. The frost had thickened on the glass the night before and closed in, until there was only a tiny peephole that permitted them to see a narrow swatch of snow and trees and the icebound lake.

It must have turned colder during the night, Del reasoned. There was a chill in the far corners of the room that hadn't been there the night before, and the wind semed to be blowing with a new viciousness. Maybe George would forget about going out to catch the one who was stealing from his traps, at least for the next day or two.

But that was not to be.

Del and Doug were about to sit down to breakfast, when the Indian boy came back into the little house, stamping the snow off his rubbers and mukluks.

"Well, it's all set." Anticipation sparkled in his eyes. "I got permission from the man who owns the cabin on my trapline for us to use it for a few days. We can go out there this morning."

Del glanced quickly at his brother, and then back

at their new friend. "You don't mean you want to go out in the bush *now*, do you? As cold as it is?"

"It isn't any colder on the trapline than it is here in the village." His logic was simple and direct. "We've got to hurry so we'll be able to do what we want to and be back before the plane comes for you."

Del wanted to ask dozens of questions. He was curious to know what they were going to do, and how they would be able to catch the thief on his trapline; but the Indian boy's eyes warned him to remain silent. It was not until they were outside in their heavy parkas that he talked about the missing skins.

"I was afraid you might say something in the house about why we were going out trapping."

Doug grinned. "We didn't think you'd want everybody to know about it."

"You can say that again." His brown eyes narrowed. "You aren't afraid to help me look for the guy who's stealing my furs, are you?"

"Oh, no." Del spoke quickly. "I'm not afraid of *looking* for the guy. I'm just afraid that we'll *find* him."

"You *bet* we'll find him! And when we do, he'll be sorry!"

George Aubichon got his .22 rifle, a box of cartridges, and the toboggan he used to pull his food and supplies over the snow. He and the boys left the isolated Indian village a short time later, following the ax-blazed trail into the woods, which people there call the "bush." The cold was bitter, but Del and Doug tried not to let it bother them.

"We'll go over and dump the gear in the cabin first," the Indian boy said.

"Then what?" Doug wanted to know.

George continued to plod forward on his snowshoes, as he told them what he planned to do. "Then we'll build a blind in the thickest bush near the beaver set where I lost two skins. That's the best place to hide and wait for him." He looked from one to the other. "How does that sound to you?"

"Great," Doug exclaimed. "But, what're we going to do if we should catch the person?"

George shrugged off the question. "We'll worry about that later. First we catch him stealing from my traps."

"That's just what I was afraid of," Doug muttered to himself. "We'll catch him and find out that we've got more than we can handle."

"Don't worry about that. If we catch him, I'll handle him, all right."

The boys pushed their way over the new snow that was piled in deep drifts across one end of the lake. Reaching the opposite shore, they angled into the bush and followed a small snow-hidden band of ice, that was a narrow, twisting stream. An hour later, they reached a little trapping cabin set back in the trees, a tiny shack with snow piled high around it.

Del turned to his brother. "That sure looks like Barney's place, doesn't it?"

"His cabin's a little bigger, but that's about the only difference."

George kicked open the door and went inside. In the North, isolated cabins in the bush were never locked. And there was always wood inside, waiting for the next person who came along. It was only the work of a few minutes for them to get their things moved in and to build a roaring fire in the airtight heater. After that, they cut some more wood and fixed something to eat. When all of the work was done, there was still time enough for them to set some of the traps before darkness ended the short winter day.

"We didn't see any sign of your thief," Del said hopefully, when they were sitting around the stove that night. "Maybe he's gone somewhere else."

"Oh, no," George replied. "He'll be back. Just as soon as I set my traps out and start getting beaver and mink again, he'll show up. Don't you worry."

Doug frowned. Who was worrying that the character wouldn't come around?

The following morning, Del and Doug helped George Aubichon set out the rest of the traps he had brought along. It was slow, cold work securing the traps in places the beaver and mink frequented, and hiding them well enough to deceive the wily, suspicious animals. When they finally had all the traps out, they built a blind big enough for the three of them at the beaver set the Indian boy claimed was the best.

"I've had three or four beaver skins from here this winter," he told them, "and twice I've had this set robbed. It's the place the thief is going to hit first."

"Maybe we should have built our blind somewhere else," Doug muttered.

George eyed him questioningly. "What'd you say?"

"Nothing. Nothing at all."

Del Davis inspected the blind carefully. It was surprising to him how cleverly George had been able to camouflage their hiding place. He knew exactly where it was, but he still had trouble seeing it a dozen paces away. Snow blended with snow to completely mask the place where they would be lying in wait for the thief.

"There," he said, "I guess that's taken care of."

"Now, all we do is come back here and wait to see who comes around to steal my pelts." George

wasn't aware of the tenseness in his voice, or the
fact that he was speaking in a hoarse whisper. "He's
not going to see us until it's too late! Then we'll
have him!"

"Maybe and maybe not."

"What do you mean by that?"

"There's the little matter of latching onto that
thief after we see him. You aren't forgetting that,
are you?"

"We'll catch him, all right; don't you worry
about that." George was confident, if nothing else.

"And what if we do?" Doug had hinted to him
once or twice about the problem they might face
with their thief. Now, however, he decided it was
too late for hinting. He and Del had to know exactly what George was planning, if they didn't want
to get into a mess that was too big for them to handle. "It just might be a good idea for us to know
what's going to happen if we do catch him."

George tugged at the lobe of his ear. "To tell
you the truth, I don't know what we'll do. I haven't
got around to figuring that out yet."

The Davis brothers eyed each other uneasily.
Doug snorted. "To tell *you* the truth, I hope we
don't run into this thief of yours."

"What's the matter?" George wanted to know.
"Are you scared?"

Doug nodded. "Right now, man, I'm scared to death, and I don't care who knows it."

The Indian lad hesitated as though he hadn't expected such honesty. "Give me a little time. I'll think of something."

"You'd better come up with some idea of how to handle him, or we'll all three be in big trouble if we do catch him."

They talked about the matter once more that night, discussing several possibilities. "I wish we had a camera along," Del said, "then we could take a picture of the guy and give it to the RCMP."

George didn't think much of that idea. "By the time we got word to the mounties and they rode up here to check it out, the guy could be halfway across Canada."

"I suppose you'd like for us to have a rope handy, so we could jump on him and tie him up," Doug said sarcastically.

Their new friend's eyes gleamed. "Do you think we could?"

Doug stared incredulously at him. "I believe you really mean that!"

The following day, the three boys made their way to the blind and crouched in it intently, waiting for the culprit Barney's grandson was sure would come. The weather had seemed cold enough before, but now that they were motionless, the sub-zero temperature stung their cheeks and drove through their warm clothes. It was not until darkness came that they finally gave up and went back to the cabin.

4

Four-legged Bandit

THE NEXT TWO DAYS passed slowly by on the trapline. The boys worked the traps during the day,
and at night they kept a vigil in the blind. But without success. Del and Doug began to doubt that
George had ever had anything taken out of his
traps.

"Are you *sure* you were robbed?" Del asked him.

"Like I told you," the Indian boy answered,
"there has been plenty of evidence that I've had
beaver and mink in my traps—and especially the
set where we put the blind. But when I got there,
they were gone." He gestured toward the nearest
blind. "I know I had plenty of skins in my traps
that someone is stealing."

Doug, who had drawn the responsibility of cooking that day, started to fix their evening meal. The

other two boys were crowding close to the stove, trying to coax the chill out of their bodies.

"We haven't seen any sign of the thief," Del persisted, eyeing George narrowly. He couldn't figure how their friend could gain anything by making them believe he'd been robbed if he hadn't, but there had to be some sort of an explanation.

"Maybe we'll have better luck tomorrow."

"What makes you say that?"

"I've just got a hunch, that's all." He stood up. "I tell you, that guy stole from me all the time. There's no reason why he wouldn't come back and do it again. We're going to catch him, you'll see."

The other boys both stared at him. "You don't mean we're going to keep on sitting out in that stupid blind, do you?" Doug asked from the stove.

George shrugged. "We've got to keep sitting out there if we're going to catch him."

Doug groaned inwardly. George sounded as though he was settled in for the winter. Of course they would be leaving soon, but he might freeze them to death before Danny did come back for them.

"I don't think your robber will ever come," he said aloud.

"Maybe. Maybe not. We just might be lucky enough to have him come tomorrow morning early, so we won't have to sit there all day."

Frowning, Doug turned from the stove. "Now that's what I call a happy thought. I don't know which would be worse—going out there and freezing to death or running into this thief of yours."

Early the next morning, George was up and had the fire going. Half an hour before daylight, they went out to work the traps once more. George was several paces ahead, striding with purpose along the snow-clogged path.

The wind and snow bit his face as sharply as it did his companions, and cut through his heavy clothes with the same intensity. He felt the same discomfort, but he had learned to accept the cold and pain quietly and without complaint. So he slogged along on his heavy snowshoes in the direction of the spot where he had placed his first set.

Del and Doug Davis didn't complain either, but it wasn't because they didn't want to. The cold stung their faces and seared their lungs, until each breath was a tortured effort. Their feet lost all feeling, and they didn't think they would ever be able to use their hands again. But they didn't dare complain or suggest turning back. If they did, George would think they were softer than he was and that they couldn't take it. They weren't going to have that. So they endured the agony in silence.

Before the trio reached the set, they saw that something had been caught in it. The snow around it gave mute evidence of what had happened. The drift had been trampled and packed, as though countless little feet had trampled it, and a few drops of blood gleamed against the white background.

George Aubichon groaned aloud. "Just look at that, will you? I had something in this trap, but that thief beat me to it!" He dashed forward and knelt beside the trap. Doug and Del pushed up beside him, staring intently. The Indian boy held up a few long hairs. "See! I had a mink in this one, but it was stolen!"

The Davis boys eyed each other seriously. There was no doubting what George had said. There *was* a thief, after all! George had caught a mink in the trap, and it wasn't there anymore.

Del straightened slowly, fixing his gaze on the brush beyond the trap. He acted as though he was half afraid that whoever or whatever had robbed the trap might be waiting to pounce on them as well.

"What did I tell you?" the Indian boy demanded. "That thief robbed me again! *Now* will you believe me?"

"We believe you all right." Doug spoke hesitantly. "We believe you."

"You sure didn't act like it." He bent over the trap once more. "Now, we have to find the character and catch him. We're not going to let him get away with that."

Del and Doug were examining the set at the same time. George had caught a mink in his trap, that was true, Del agreed. And it was gone, so it had either worked itself free, or someone had taken it out of the trap. But there was something strange about it; something he couldn't quite understand. Then he realized what it was. It was so stupid to have missed it, that he felt embarrassed to say anything.

"Do you guys know something?" he asked. "No *person* could have stolen your mink."

George's lower jaw sagged slightly. "And just what do you mean by that?"

"I don't see any footprints around here that would show that a man had robbed you. Something else must have happened!"

The youthful Indian scowled indignantly, eyes flashing his sudden anger. "You don't think I'm so stupid I wouldn't have thought of looking for footprints, do you?"

Del swallowed against the lump in his throat. "I didn't even think about you. I—I didn't see any footprints and so I—" His voice trailed away.

"Whoever robbed me was smart enough to do it without leaving any tracks to give himself away."

"And how would he do that?"

"He'd brush them out with a spruce bough, the way I did when we finished making our sets. After the wind had blown for a little while, or a few flakes of new snow fell, no one would be able to tell that he had ever been here."

"I guess maybe you're right," Doug acknowledged. "We just didn't think of that, did we, Del?"

The other boy started to agree reluctantly, but stopped momentarily, his sharp gaze held by something else a foot or two from the trampled snow.

"What is it?" Doug demanded.

"That's what I'd like to know." He pointed to a set of tracks in the snow. "What's this?"

George examined them carefully, eyes narrowing as he did so.

"I don't know for sure. It looks sort of like a wolf to me."

"A wolf?" Doug gasped.

"Yeh. Sometimes they come to take a look at a trap after something's been caught in it. They're real curious that way."

"You don't suppose he could have stolen your mink, do you?"

George shook his head. "Nope. He might eat half the animal, but he wouldn't take it out of the trap the way this mink was taken out." He paused for a moment, breathing heavily. "It's just like I told you. Whoever robbed my traps was on two legs, not four."

The boys looked at each other. "What are we going to do?"

"We're going to move this set, for one thing. Then we're going on and see how many more traps that thief got into."

The next two traps were just as they had been when the boys finished putting them out. But the fourth, a beaver set on the creek, had been molested. Again, George saw that there had been a visitor ahead of them.

His eyes darkened angrily. "It's happened again!" he exclaimed, desperation lacing his voice.

There were the same signs of an animal threshing about on the snow, and the same telltale marks of blood; but that was all. There was no sign of the beaver.

"Just wait until I get my hands on that character! He'll be sorry he ever stole anything from me!" He knelt beside the set and looked it over thoughtfully. "Now here's something else I can't understand."

Del and Doug squatted beside him.

"We made this set under water," he continued. "And the beaver would have drowned. There shouldn't be any blood or scuffed-up snow here." He lifted the trap. There were the telltale bits of fur again. "It just doesn't make sense."

"And here are those same wolf tracks again." Doug pointed to them.

George Aubichon's brown cheeks blanched, and concern leaped to his dark eyes.

"These aren't wolf tracks!" His voice broke. "I should have seen that before!"

"If a wolf didn't make them, what did?"

"They were made by a wolverine!"

Del and Doug Davis both gasped. A wolverine! They had heard about the cunningness of the wolverine, how it robbed traplines week after week as cleverly as any thief, and how they managed to avoid the clutches of the cleverest trappers.

"I'm done!" Dismay edged George's thin voice. "I'm finished! Until I trap that wolverine, I won't be able to get a thing from my traps!"

Doug was relieved at the new development. "At least we don't have to sit out in that blind anymore," he murmured.

George, who had been kneeling beside the trap, straightened slowly, his dark face revealing the consternation that surged violently within him. It was as though someone had stolen even the strength he needed to breathe. He felt as though he was going to collapse where he was.

"I wish it was a man!" he muttered.

"You've got to be kidding."

"I've never been more serious in my life!" he

said in desperation. "You don't know what it's like to try to catch a wolverine! They're the most difficult animals in the North to trap!"

"Maybe so!" Doug was still glad that the wolverine they were going after had four legs instead of two. At least a four-legged one wouldn't be apt to carry a gun.

5

Best Laid Plans

THERE WAS A BRIEF PAUSE, during which the boys looked at each other curiously and then down at the tracks again.

"What are you going to do now, George?" Doug Davis asked.

Numbly, the Indian boy brushed an unsteady hand across his face. "Yeh, what are we going to do?"

He shrugged. "I've never even tried to set a trap for a wolverine, but I've heard my dad talk about it. I think I know how it's done."

"Good!" Del broke in quickly. "We don't know anything about it, but if we can help you, we sure will."

George acted as though he hadn't even heard him. "It's not going to be easy. I can tell you that much. A wolverine's just about the smartest ani-

47

mal there is. Dad says they'll laugh at traps that would fool any other animal."

For the first time since they saw the beaver set and the telltale tracks, Del was aware of the cold. It drove through his heavy coat and set him to shivering. "Well, whatever we're going to do, let's get with it. There's no use standing out here freezing to death."

"I guess you're right." George stooped to take hold of the trap. "The first thing we have to do is to take up the traps and carry them back to the cabin."

This was something the boys did not understand. "I thought you wanted to try and catch that wolverine," Doug told him.

"I do. That's why we've got to bring the traps in. We'll have to boil them to remove any trace of human scent."

Doug thought George was kidding him. "You don't expect us to believe that, do you? There isn't any odor on those traps. I can't smell a thing, and I'll bet you can't either."

George answered simply, "Maybe not, but we're not wolverines."

Doug laughed. "I guess you've got a point there."

"After we boil the traps, what then?" Del wanted to know.

"We see if we can't set the traps cleverly enough to catch the wolverine."

"And if we don't?"

"I might as well quit trapping this winter. There's no use trying to buck a wolverine. He'll get most of the pelts, and I'll do all the work."

They finished covering the trapline as quickly as possible, taking up the traps and putting them on the toboggan they had brought along in case there were any skins to take back. By noon they had finished the job and were back at the cabin again.

Once there, Doug and Del helped the Indian boy carry a big kettle from the ramshackle lean-to porch and fill it with snow. By midafternoon they had boiled the traps long enough to remove the human scent.

"There," George murmured, "that ought to be done enough."

"I'll help you get the kettle off the stove."

Once that was accomplished, they took the traps out of the boiling water, using a stick the Indian boy brought in from the outside. Using a piece of soft cloth, he picked up the traps by their chains and hung them on the line that was stretched across a corner of the cabin.

"We've finished with that job," Del said, doubt creeping into his voice, "but do you think it'll do any good?"

"If we don't touch them, it will. The wolverine has a keen nose. He can pick up the slightest trace of human scent, and he's smart enough to know that men mean trouble for him."

Del scratched his head. "If he's that smart, I don't see how we'll be able to make a set that's clever enough to fool him."

"It's not easy," George agreed. "It's sure not easy."

The following morning, they took the traps out to the trapline on the toboggan and put them out once more. Although Doug and Del went along the same as usual, George insisted on doing everything himself. "It's really got to be done right," he explained.

They watched with interest as he worked, even more slowly than before. It was late in the afternoon when he finished putting out the last of the traps and used a pine bough to brush out his tracks.

"Now that job's over," George said with satisfaction.

"Do you think this'll do it?" Doug put in, turning to face their Indian companion. "Do you think we'll catch the wolverine tomorrow?"

George snorted. "I'll be lucky if I get him in a month." With that he glanced up at the lowering skies. "Now, if we're lucky, we'll get a little snow tonight to cover our tracks better and help hide the traps more than they're hidden now."

He had his wish about the snow. It started coming down once more, even before they made it back to the cabin. And by the time they were inside again and had the fire rebuilt, half an inch of new snow had fallen. That made George feel better. He began to laugh and joke a little; and when they talked with him about the possibilities of getting the wolverine, he seemed to be more optimistic.

"And as soon as we do, I'll be all set. I'll catch plenty of beaver and mink and 'rats." His grin was crooked, and excitement danced in his dark eyes. "Then I'll be able to make enough money to go down to Saskatoon and get a job where I can make some of that big money."

"What kind of a job?" Doug asked. He really hadn't intended to pose such a personal question, but he was so surprised to learn that the Indian boy was planning on leaving the North, that the question popped out without bidding.

George stared blankly at him. He wasn't angry because Doug had asked him something so personal—just surprised. The kind of a job he would be getting had never really occurred to him.

"I don't know," he admitted, "but Saskatoon's a big place. There's a lot of work around there."

"It's a big place, all right," Del put in, "but a

lot of people live there, too. You might find it isn't quite as easy to get a job as you think it is."

"A friend of mine went down there to work. When he came back last fall, he said that jobs are easy to find. He says all you have to do is go around and find out all the different places where they need workers and how much they'll pay. Then you can pick out the one you like the best and work there."

It was some time before either of the boys answered him.

"Maybe you'll find it that way," Doug finally said. "But I don't know whether I'd want to depend on getting a job so easy. It sure isn't like that back in Fairview where we live. Del and I tried for weeks to get work, and we never did find anything steady. All we could get were a few odd jobs."

"That's right. I wouldn't want to go somewhere and get a job that wouldn't pay me enough to live on. There aren't very many jobs that I'd be qualified to do."

George airily brushed aside their appraisal of the job situation. "I don't have to worry about that. My friend says there're lots of jobs. I'll look him up, and he'll help me."

They didn't say anything more. They didn't know but that he was right about finding work in the Canadian city to the south. They had only been there once, themselves. But they were quite sure it wasn't quite as easy to find work as George thought it would be.

"I'm going down and get a job," he repeated, "and a good place to stay. Then I'm going to get me a big motorcycle and a car and have some fun. I'm tired of living up here where a guy can't do anything!"

Doug and Del nodded. They both knew what George meant. There were times when they dreamed about the day when they could get a car of their own or a pair of motorcycles and travel around the country. Once they had even talked about saving their money and trying to get something of their own as soon as they were old enough to drive. Only they knew that they really couldn't. They didn't have the money for a car or a motorcycle and insurance and taxes and repairs, for one thing.

For another, they were sure Danny would object. He was different than some parents about things like that. They thought he was old-fashioned, but they didn't say anything about it. In a way they were glad that he cared enough about them to refuse to allow them to do just anything they wanted to.

The next morning, the boys went out to look at the traps, but there was no sign of the wolverine.

The next day, it was obvious that he had visited

the traps first. Two sets had mink taken from them, and there was no doubt as to what had happened. The wolverine had left abundant evidence that it had been there. George's discouragement continued to grow.

"I tell you, we've got to catch that guy! If we don't, we might as well take up our traps and go back to the village. I'm not going to be able to do anything with my trapline until he's out of the way."

Del Davis felt the same as their new Indian friend about the futility of staying on the trapline as long as the wolverine was there, but he tried to sound optimistic about their chances of trapping the wily raider.

"Maybe we'll have him in the next trap," he said hopefully.

"Yeh," George retorted irritably. "Maybe we will. And maybe we won't, either. I'm beginning to think that we'll *never* trap that character."

They went on to the next trap, trying not to show their consternation. The third trap was sprung, but there was no sign that anything had ever been in it.

"Look at that," Del said. "Whatever was in this trap got away."

"This is a new development." Doug picked up

the trap with his heavily mittened hand. "There's no sign of blood or hair or anything."

George Aubichon took it from him. "It's that wolverine!" The words exploded from his lips. "He just set off that trap to show me how little he's afraid of me and my trapping!" He muttered something else in Cree that the boys couldn't understand, and threw the trap over his shoulder.

"What're we going to do now?" Doug wanted to know. There seemed to be a finality in what George had done, as though they had reached the end of everything. "Are we going to quit trapping?"

"I haven't decided yet." He started up the trail, shoving his snowshoes through the new drifts. "But that's about the only thing I can think of to do until that wolverine is out of the way."

"*If* he's out of the way," Del murmured. "The way it looks to me, we're going to have a mighty rough time getting him."

"That's what I've been trying to tell you." He breathed deeply. "Somehow I left some sign on the traps that had shown him a man has been around."

"Maybe we ought to boil the traps again and be a little more careful in handling them."

The boys gathered up the rest of the traps and started back to the cabin. The trip seemed to be even longer and colder than it had been before. The Davis boys couldn't help feeling sorry for

George. He was so terribly upset by the wolverine and the fact that he hadn't been able to trap the wily animal. They wished they knew enough about trapping to help him, but they didn't. About all they could do was to go along and keep him company and do the things he asked them to do.

They were still fifty yards from the little trapping cabin, when Del noticed that the door was open.

"Look!" He groaned aloud. "We must've forgotten to close the door when we left this morning."

"Forgot, nothing!" George cried. He ran forward, moving as fast as he could on his snowshoes. Doug and Del were two steps behind him. He stopped suddenly, his lower jaw sagging and his lithe frame going limp. It was a moment before he could speak.

"Take a squint at that, would you!"

The Davis boys stared incredulously into the dark interior of the cabin. At first they could scarcely believe that what they were seeing was real. But it was! All too real!

The cabin, that had been so clean when they left that morning, was a shambles. The stove had been turned over and ashes and soot strewn across the floor, mingling with the flour that had been knocked off the small cupboard and scattered about with demonic abandon. The glass in the little window had been broken out, and dishes, silver, and cooking utensils had been thrown on the floor.

"What happened?" Del had difficulty forcing out the words. He had never seen such complete destruction. "Who would come in and wreck your place this way?"

"That's what I'd like to know," Doug said.

"It was that wolverine!" The way George pronounced the word, it was almost profanity. "He must have smelled our bacon, and he came in to get it!"

"Now wait a minute," Doug countered. "Don't kid us that way. No animal could come in and wreck a cabin the way this one's wrecked. Some person did it."

"That shows you don't know much about wolverines. I told you they're smart. And they're destructive too! They'll do 'most anything."

Del took off his snowshoes and went into the cabin. It proved to be even worse than they had thought at first. Every ounce of food they brought with them, except for a few canned vegetables, had been destroyed.

"Man!" he exclaimed. "It looks as though a baby cyclone went through here!"

"You can say that again!"

For a minute, the boys stood in silence just inside the doorway, surveying the damage to the little cabin. At last Doug directed his attention to their Indian friend.

"Now what do we do?" he asked.

"What *can* we do?" George's disappointment was keen. "We don't have any food left and nothing to eat it off of, if we did. The only thing we can do now is pack up and go home."

"No wonder you said that you've got to get that wolverine out of here before you'll be able to do any more trapping," Del said. "I've never seen anything like this before. It looks as though an atomic bomb went off in there."

George very soberly replied, "I've heard my dad and some of the older hunters talk about the wol-verines and the damage they can do on a trapline and in a cabin. But I can tell you this much right now—I sure didn't know it could be this bad."

6

Defeat and Retreat

THE BOYS loaded their traps and sleeping bags on the toboggan and started back to the village. George shuffled through the snow a half dozen paces ahead of them, his head down. He didn't talk to either of them for almost a half hour.

"I sure feel bad about the way things turned out, don't you?" Del asked, speaking softly enough so the Indian boy could not hear what he was saying. "George is sure shook up about this, and I can't say that I blame him. He won't be able to trap any more this winter, if that wolverine hangs around his trapline and he isn't able to catch him."

Doug nodded.

"I feel sorry for him too, but maybe it's a good thing that it's all working out this way."

Del looked up quickly, questions gleaming in his eyes. "What makes you say that?"

"If he isn't able to make any money with his traps this winter, he might not be able to save enough money to pay his way to Saskatoon to look for work."

Del thought over what his brother had said. In a way, Doug did make a lot of sense. If George had good luck trapping and went down to Saskatoon, he could have worse problems.

"His folks wouldn't let him go there to work. He isn't any older than we are."

"Or, maybe he'd run away if they said he couldn't go south," Del added.

"I think you're right. Anyway, I'm positive that George would get down to Saskatoon one way or another, if he is able to scrape together enough money to make the trip. He thinks that once he's there, he's got it made. He can have everything he's ever wanted."

George hadn't changed his mind about going to Saskatoon. Indeed, when they stopped to rest for a few minutes, he had new plans for getting to Saskatoon right away.

"I have an idea that might help me to work things out, anyway. About getting down to Saskatoon, I mean."

They waited for him to continue.

"If you'll promise not to tell anybody, I'll tell you what it is."

They both looked up and nodded, but that wasn't assurance enough for him that they would remain silent. "You won't say anything to my grandfather or anyone else about this, will you?"

"We won't say a word," Doug replied.

George leaned forward, excitement smiling in his dark face. "I've just decided something that will work out just about as well as catching that wolverine and trapping all winter. A guy tried to buy my traps the other day. I think I'll hunt him up when we get back to the village and sell them to him."

This surprised them. "You mean you're quitting the trapline for good?" Doug blurted.

"The way I look at it, I might as well. With the money I get from my traps I can go to Saskatoon right away and get that good paying job, so I can buy myself a motorcycle and a car."

The boys' eyes widened. "You wouldn't let that wolverine get the best of you, would you?" Doug asked.

"Why not? I've tried and tried to catch him, but I haven't even been able to come close."

Del had to agree with him that it didn't look as though he could ever catch the wolverine.

"And I'm not going to make anything on my trapping as long as that pest is out there waiting to steal anything I do get. The way I see it, I might as well quit and go right away."

Doug asked the question that had been on his mind ever since George first talked about going south to get a job. "Will your folks let you go?"

The Indian boy shrugged indifferently. "Dad's going away in a few days and won't be back for another two or three months, and my stepmother doesn't care what I do. To tell you the truth, I think she'd be glad to have me out of the way. Then she wouldn't have to worry about feeding me."

Doug and Del were incredulous. "She sure doesn't seem to be that kind to me," Del said.

"The trouble is that you don't know her the way I do. She's real nice to me when someone else is around, but you ought to see how things are when we're alone. It's not like having a real mother."

Doug had to take issue with him on that. "Del and I don't have a real mother, either. She and Dad were drowned on the mission field in Guatemala, and we live with Danny and Kay Orlis. But I can tell you this, they love us too much to let us do just as we please. And they sure wouldn't let us drop out of school and go off to a city to get a job."

George got to his feet and took hold of the rope on the toboggan. He was ready to continue the cold, tiring trip back to the village.

"I'm sixteen. I can leave school any time I want to. I don't have to pay any attention to what anybody says. And Dad wouldn't stop me from going to Saskatoon, even if he were here. I can do what I want."

Del broke in. "You mean he wouldn't say *anything* about your going off to a place like Saskatoon alone?"

George snorted. "Like I said, I do as I please. I don't have to ask anybody about anything."

He acted as though it didn't make any difference how many people knew he was going to Saskatoon to get a job, nobody would say anything. Yet, before they went on, he made them give him their word again that they wouldn't tell on him. Reluctantly, they agreed to keep silent.

"But I still think you're making a big mistake," Del told him.

"I didn't ask you what you thought about it, did I?"

They got back to the village that night half an hour after dark, so weary that after they had something to eat, they went off to bed.

In spite of the fact that they were very tired, Del and Doug talked in whispers for a long while before sleep claimed them.

"I sure think George is making a terrible mistake," Del said. "I wish there was something we could do about it."

"Me, too."

"He's not going to be able to find a job in Saskatoon. It'd be hard enough for a guy his age to get work if he'd already graduated from high school."

"You can say that again. He's only sixteen and hasn't finished the tenth grade yet. He's going to be in real trouble."

There was a short silence, then Del broke it. "I'll bet Barney wouldn't let him go if he knew about it."

"He sure wouldn't. And neither would his folks, the way I get it. If they would, he wouldn't have to keep everything such a big secret."

"But we can't tell Barney or George's dad or anyone what he's planning. We promised him that we wouldn't say anything."

Doug raised on one elbow momentarily. "Yeh, I was just thinking that. It was a stupid thing to do, wasn't it?"

"Maybe so, but we can't go back on our word."

"About all we can do right now is pray about it."

The temperature plunged to new lows during the night and hunkered there, keeping the mercury in the bulb of the thermometer. The cold filled the air with ice crystals as fine as fog. They cut the visibility to a hundred yards. Doug and Del noticed that a cold wave had come in, as soon as they got up.

"One thing I'm sure about. We don't have to worry about going anywhere today, except maybe out in the yard for some more wood," Doug said, shivering as he pulled on his trousers.

"I'm glad we're not out on that trapline. George would have us out checking traps the same as usual."

The boys were sure they would get to stay in by the fire all day, but they reckoned without Barney Aubichon. Shortly after breakfast, he came over to his son's house, his cardboard suitcase in his stubby fist.

A grin split his wrinkled face when he saw his grandson and the Davis boys back from the trapline.

"I didn't expect you boys home quite so soon," he said. "I thought you were going to be spending the whole week on your trapline, George." His eyes gleamed. "Or did the bears scare you away?"

His grandson scowled at him, as though he meant something personal by what he said. "It wasn't the bears that made us come home," he retorted testily. "It was that stupid wolverine! He ruined everything."

Barney chuckled. He had a way of laughing

when adversity came. It was almost as though the laughter helped to lighten the load.

"Don't tell me that you've got wolverine troubles on your trapline!" He laughed again, his broad, booming voice filling the cabin.

George hadn't yet reached the place where he could laugh when things went wrong. The frown lines about his face deepened.

"I know it isn't so funny to you, George, but I can't help laughing when I think what a wolverine can do to a trapline or a trapping cabin. I've had it happen to me. Let me tell you that!" He chuckled again, clasping his hands about his big stomach. "You know, I used to say that Satan, himself, was the only one who could make a wolverine as cantankerous and ornery as he is."

The Indian boy went over and sat down near his grandfather. The fact that Barney felt the way he did about wolverines seemed to forge a bond between them, because George realized the old man understood what it was like to have his traps robbed and his cabin and supplies ruined.

"Did you ever get rid of your wolverine?" he asked.

Barney nodded. "I got rid of him, but it wasn't easy. I can tell you that. It wasn't easy."

"How did you do it?"

The old man's small eyes squinted. "How did

you try to get rid of your wolverine, George?" he asked.

"I figured I'd have to trap him, so I boiled my traps and made my sets as carefully as I ever saw Dad make his; but that old wolverine must have spotted something that wasn't right. He didn't even come close to getting caught."

Barney chuckled, but this time his grandson didn't mind it. He knew his grandfather was laughing with him.

"I'll bet he set your traps off, eh?" he asked.

His grandson stared at him. "How did you know that?"

"That's the way my wolverine used to do me. I got so mad at him, I could've wrung his neck! I had the idea that he was laughing at me. I figured he was sittin' out there behind a bush laughin' his head off when he saw me come to look in my trap."

George nodded.

After a time his grandfather spoke again, quietly. "You wouldn't by any chance like to have some help trying to trap that thief of yours, would you?"

Doug and Del thought George would be excited about the prospect of having his grandfather's help, but instead he scowled at him.

"We couldn't catch him," he muttered.

"Maybe not, but I'd sure like to give it a try." Barney laid his finger alongside his broad nose thoughtfully. "I've got a trick or two that just might work."

"He's the smartest animal I've ever tried to trap," George said, as though he thought it was impossible for his grandfather to be wise enough to catch the wolverine either.

"That's fine with me. I like to take on a battle like that." Barney's stomach shook with laughter. "You whip a wolverine and you know you've really done something!"

But the boy acted as though the old man's assistance would be valueless. "I don't figure there's any use for us to try to catch that wolverine now, Grandpa. You should see the way he messed things up."

Barney's eyes slitted narrowly, and for a time he studied the hurt that darkened the face of his young grandson. He understood how George felt. He would feel the same himself, if he were trapping and a wolverine moved in on him. But he couldn't let George lay down without a fight. He had to learn to face trouble and conquer it.

"You mean you're going to quit?" Scorn honed his voice. "Are you going to let that wolverine get the best of you?"

The boy shrugged defensively. "I figure I might just as well sell my traps and let someone else fight with him."

7

One More Try

THE DAY WORE ON monotonously. The snow, that
had been coming down in brief flurries since Barney Aubichon came, had almost ceased; but the
clouds seemed to press down against the isolated
little village, and the wind gave evidence of building. It must have grown colder outside. The airtight heater seemed to do an even poorer job of
heating the cabin than usual, and the frost thickened on the windows.

Barney said little to George about the wolverine
and his trapline until they had finished dinner and
were sitting around the table. The old Indian sat
motionless, his pudgy hands resting on his stomach
and his fingers clasped together. His eyes narrowed,
until Del thought perhaps he had fallen asleep.
Then he stirred himself.

"You know, George, the first time I ran up

against a wolverine, I reckon I was just about your age. For all I remember, I might even have been working the same trapline you're on." The corners of his mouth tilted upward, as he thought back to the time when he was a boy, trapping the way his grandson was doing.

"Anyway, I had to pick up my traps and come home. I was going to quit, too. I had decided there was nothing I could do to catch that wolverine. He had whipped me good. I guess I was just about as discouraged as you are right now."

George moistened his lips thoughtfully. That surprised him. He had always thought of his grandfather as a person who could do almost anything. "Then, what did you do?" he asked.

"Well, my dad wouldn't let me quit. He made me go out and fight the wolverine on his own ground. We boiled my traps and took them back, and I set them again."

"And I suppose you got your wolverine right off," George said, his disgust showing through.

"I wish it had been that easy. I thought I had followed directions carefully, but I must have made a mistake someplace. I still didn't get them right, and the wolverine still had the best of me."

"Did you quit, then?" George wanted to know.

"I wanted to quit," his grandfather continued. "Believe me, I wanted to. I didn't think there was any use in going out and trying again. I said the same thing you did. If that old wolverine wanted the trapline so bad, as far as I was concerned, he could have it." Barney chuckled. "Only I wasn't going to trap for him. He'd have to get his mink and beaver for himself. But Dad wouldn't let me give up. He made me go back."

"A lot of good that'd do with *this* wolverine. He doesn't act like an animal at all. He acts like a *person!*"

"I know. I know. But there're ways of catching him, just like there were ways of catching my wolverine. My dad showed me what I was doing wrong, and even helped me make the first set so he'd be sure I understood how. That time we got results. I took care of old Mr. Wolverine. He didn't rob any more traps after *I* finished with him."

George thought about that. He did want to go to Saskatoon and had almost convinced himself that he would make enough money off his traps to make the trip. But, it would be a lot better, he reasoned, to go out and finish off the wolverine so he could trap the rest of the season. Then he'd have a lot more money to use for going to Saskatoon to find work. If he sold his traps, he would get barely enough for them to pay his fare.

"So you think I ought to go out and try again, eh?"

Barney's eyes narrowed. "If you're not scared to, I sure do."

George's eyes flashed. "I'm not scared of him. I can tell you that much."

The old man nodded approvingly.

"But I don't know how to make a better set than I've been doing, and that's the truth." He paused. "Will you tell me how to set out my traps so the wolverine won't spot them?"

"I'll do better than that. I'll go along with you and help you trap him."

His grandson hesitated. "You wouldn't have to do that."

"It's better that way. I can tell you, but that doesn't mean you'll understand everything I say. I've learned a thing or two about wolverines since that time when I had so much trouble. They're clever, but the wolverine hasn't lived who's smart enough to fool me."

Del and Doug glanced quickly at the elderly Indian. They were surprised to hear him bragging; but after they thought about it, they decided he wasn't bragging at all. He was confident that he knew enough about trapping to outwit the animal that was pestering his grandson. And that was that.

The boys thought George would be eager for the old man's help, but he didn't seem to be. "You don't have to go with us, Grandpa. You can tell us what to do."

A grin crinkled Barney's brown face. He didn't seem to catch the reluctance in his grandson's manner. "It so happens that I want to go with you, George." He sighed deeply. "It's been a long, long time since I've been on a Saskatchewan trapline. I've got a hankering to get out on the trail for a few days and see if I can trap as well as I think I can."

Barney didn't ask if George wanted him to go. He just assumed that he did and happily went ahead with his plans for going back to the trapping cabin with his grandson and the Davis boys.

George was still fuming about it when he took Del and Doug with him later in the afternoon to feed their dogs.

"I don't know why he's got to go with us," he muttered. "It's sure not goin' to be any fun to have *him* along."

Del spoke quickly. He couldn't let old Barney go undefended. "I don't know about that. Your granddad knows an awful lot about animals and birds. I can tell you this much right now. If it were my trapline, I'd want to have him along. I'd learn a lot from him."

George kicked a chunk of hard snow with his mukluks, wincing at the sharp pain that shot up his ankle. "If he just wanted to get that wolverine, it would be all right. But that isn't the reason he wants to go with us. That's just his excuse."

"I don't know about that."

"He wants to go along so he can have a better chance of preaching at me."

Doug didn't agree with him. "I think you're wrong about that. All he wants to do is help you get your wolverine so you can begin to trap mink and beaver again."

George shook his head. "He's got you fooled the same as everybody else. But he doesn't fool me. Other people just don't know him as well as I do." Anger flecked his brown eyes. "I was glad when he moved to the States. I got a little rest from all his preaching, then."

Doug would have replied, but somehow it didn't seem to be the time for him to mention spiritual things. George was too upset, too much on the defensive.

Barney may have known that his grandson didn't want him to go with them on the trapline. As far as Del and Doug could observe, the elderly Indian missed little of what went on around him, although he often kept silent. But if he knew of George's displeasure, he chose to ignore it. The next morning he got his bedroll and some food together and prodded the boys to get ready, so they could go out to the trapping cabin as soon as possible.

"We've got a lot of work to do out there before the place is fit to live in again," he said. "We'll go out this morning and get the cabin cleaned up. Then we'll see about boiling the traps and making the sets so we can catch old Mr. Wolverine for you."

George Aubichon glared at his grandfather, but he did not protest. He knew it would do no good for him to say that he didn't want his granddad to go with them. Barney had made up his mind to help him with his traps. Nothing anyone could say would change him on that.

The only indication there was that the young Indian didn't like having his grandfather along when they left the village, was the fact that he said little on the long, cold trip out to the trapline. It didn't seem to the Davis boys that it took nearly as long for them to get to the cabin this time as it had when they first went out. Before they realized they had covered half the distance, they saw the little building through the trees.

"There it is," George said. "Just like we left it."

Barney was chuckling jovially, as he opened the cabin door and squinted inside. "Just look at that!" His laughter rang. "Any trapper in the country could take one look at the inside of this cabin and know that a wolverine had come calling. That's for sure. There isn't another animal anywhere in the

North that can do so much damage in so short a time."

George was grumbling under his breath. "You aren't telling me anything new."

Barney straightened, ignoring his grandson's remark.

"Well, I guess we'd better get busy. Our work's cut out for us, if we want to get this cabin cleaned up enough to live in for the next few days."

They built a fire in the little stove and set to work. With four of them on the job, it was only an hour or so until the cabin was as clean as ever. Barney boiled the traps once more. He did it in much the same way as George had done, except that he was more careful to remove the last remnant of human scent.

"I *did* all of that," the boy said impatiently, "but it didn't help any. The wolverine still spotted my traps."

Barney kept right on working. "This is one of the most important parts of the job. I'll show you how to get rid of *all* human scent. Then, if you watch real close, I'll show you how to make a good wolverine set." His eyes flashed. "We'll get that animal before we quit. You'll see."

On the trapline, Del and Doug watched the old Indian carefully, as he made the sets for the clever trap robber. In general, it seemed that he did everything in almost the same way that George had done. Only, when he finished, there was no sign of the trap anywhere. It was as though it had suddenly vanished. The boys had watched him place the trap, so they knew where it was; but even with that advantage, they could make out no sign of it.

Barney brushed over his tracks with careful attention to each minute spot of snow and even carried the branch he used as a broom some distance away.

"Man, oh man!" Del exclaimed. "Did you ever see anything like that? It's a good thing I'm not a wolverine. It'd fool me."

George snorted his indignation. "I did all the same things."

"Yeh, but not like Barney did them. A set like this one'd fool anything!"

"It's no better than mine," he murmured.

Neither of the boys agreed and told him so. "You didn't get the wolverine," they pointed out.

"Grandpa hasn't gotten him, either. Don't forget that."

"You just wait. He will."

George was fuming inwardly when they went back to the cabin. He kept muttering to himself, as Del and Doug talked about the way his grandfather had set the traps and how sure they were that he was going to trap the wolverine in a day or two.

"I'd have gotten him myself if we hadn't had to go home for some more supplies," the Indian boy protested. "You don't need to think Grandpa is the only one who knows how to set traps."

"But you've got to admit that they're better than any set you ever made," Del said, laughing. "I don't suppose there's anyone in the village who can trap the way Barney can."

George said no more about it; but all through the evening meal, he lowered angrily.

That night, as soon as supper was over, Barney Aubichon took out his Bible and began to read aloud to his three companions. It was the sort of thing he had done many times when Del and Doug visited him in his little cabin in Minnesota. They had always been glad for it. However, George sat there during the reading, staring into the fire with hostile eyes. And when his grandfather bowed his head for prayer, George stared straight ahead.

Barney thanked God for allowing him and the Davis boys to come back to his northern Saskatchewan home to visit his family. He thanked Him for the privilege of being back on the trapline for a few days and asked Him to help them to catch the wolverine. And he prayed for his grandson.

"You know George isn't a Christian," he said as simply as though he was talking to someone sitting in the chair across from him. "You know that he has never confessed his sin and put his trust in You to save him. Dear God, please help him to see his need of letting You have complete control. Help him to see that You love him and want to save him."

Barney continued to pray, but his grandson was no longer listening. He might have expected something like this, he told himself angrily. His granddad couldn't get him alone and talk with him. He had to do it out in the open, in front of Del and Doug. Well, he didn't care what the old man wanted. He was going to live his own life. Nobody was going to tell him what to do!

Even if George had been told, he would not have believed that his grandfather was so used to talking with the Lord that he was never aware of anyone else who may have been listening.

As soon as Barney finished praying, George pushed back from the table, noisily, and got to his feet.

"Where're you going?" Barney asked mildly.

"I don't know, but I can tell you this much! I'd like to get out of here!"

8

George's Boner

IT WAS ALWAYS COLD in the middle of the winter in
northern Saskatchewan. No one expected anything
else. But it seemed colder than ever in the little
trapping cabin that particular night. Usually there
was little wind, especially when the mercury stayed
in the bottom of the tube, but that night was an
exception.

A sharp, bitter wind with snow in its teeth,
swirled about the cabin. It leaked through the
cracks between the logs and rattled the window in
the casing. As it did so, it drove the feeble circle of
heat ever closer to the little wood stove.

The boys and Barney sat up for a time playing
Chinese checkers and talking about the North.
George joined the others, but it was obvious that
he was upset. He seldom talked, and smiled not at

all. He was the first to decide he'd had enough of
the game for one night.

"I don't care what the rest of you guys do, but
I'm goin' to bed," he blurted.

Barney consulted his watch. "It might not be a
bad idea. We've got a lot of things to do tomorrow.
We might as well get a good night's sleep so we'll be
ready for anything that comes in the morning."

"Like catching the wolverine?" Doug asked.

"Yeh. Like catching the wolverine."

Before midnight, the fire went out, and the water
in the pail in the corner froze a thick layer of ice
over the top. Del and Doug snuggled deep in their
sleeping bags, ignoring the wind and the cold. They
were thankful that they didn't have to be outside
on such a miserable night.

For some reason Doug found it quite difficult to
get to sleep. He lay there for an hour or more
thinking about Danny Orlis, who was in the same
general area to do some flying for the mission. They
hadn't had radio contact with him since he left, but
there was no doubt in Doug's mind that Danny was
weathered in someplace. He had told them repeat-
edly about being grounded by the weather and how
he had to wait it out.

He would have to wait until the weather cleared,
before he finished the flying he came to do. That
would likely mean that they wouldn't be back in

Fairview in time for school to take up when the midwinter vacation was over and classes started again.

Doug really didn't mind missing school all that much. In fact it would be sort of nice, except for the fact that they would have a lot of work to make up. That was the thing that threw him. They'd have to take books home every night and study like anything just to get caught up with the rest of the kids. And that could be rough. He'd had to do it before.

For a long while Doug lay there thinking about school and home back in Fairview. Everything seemed so far away, so unreal. It was almost as though their other life was only a dream that had existed in memory, and the North and the cold were all that were genuine.

After what seemed to be half the night, he closed his eyes and finally drifted off to sleep. It was almost morning when he stirred restlessly, caught in that never-never land between sleep and wakefulness. Doug opened his eyes and stared into the opaque blackness above him, unable to remember for a time where he was and what he was doing there.

Realization came slowly, and with it a vague uneasiness. He didn't know why, but it seemed as though he was sure something terrible was about

to happen. Doug reached over to the bedroll beside him and felt for Del. His brother was there,
his back turned to him, still sound asleep.

It's silly to be so upset, Doug told himself. He
probably felt the way he did because he had been
thinking about school and Kay and DeeDee and the
kids back home. He had never been homesick before, but he had to admit that could be the problem.

Whether it was or not, he reasoned, there was no
use in letting himself get so uptight about it. They
would be going back home in a few days; and when
they got there, he and Del would probably wish
they were back on the trapline with Barney and
George. But he doubted it.

Nevertheless, before trying to go back to sleep,
he reached for the Indian boy, his fingers groping
for the other sleeping bag. He was sure he would
find George sleeping about the same distance away
as Del was, only on the other side.

But George was not there.

Doug reached frantically for him. His sleeping
bag was there, but he was gone! A thin gasp shook
Doug's body.

Doug jerked upright in his sleeping bag, staring
numbly into the darkness, as he tried to see the far
corners of the log building. His first thought was
that George had felt cold and got up to rebuild the

fire. That had happened on other occasions when they were in the trapping cabin. One or the other had decided they had to have a little more heat.

But usually, when that happened, it was with a flashlight and noise enough to waken everyone. This time there hadn't been a sound.

Doug tried to pierce the darkness with his eyes, but that was impossible. And all he could hear was the steady breathing of Barney and Del.

"George!" Doug called out in a hoarse whisper. "George!"

No answer.

"George!"

Del stirred, his brother's voice coming to him from somewhere far away. "What's the matter?" he demanded sleepily. "What's wrong?"

"It's George! He's not here!"

Del jerked erect, his eyes widening. He had heard Doug clearly, but there had to be some mistake.

"What?"

"He's gone!"

By this time, Barney was awake too. He sat up slowly, squinting at the boys in the semidarkness. "Are you sure?"

"Look for yourself! I woke up and felt for him and—and he was gone." Doug unzipped his sleeping bag and crawled out, shivering in the cold.

The elderly Indian took charge of the situation calmly. "We'd better get a light and some heat in here." He struck a match and touched the feeble flame to the kerosene wick. He would have built a fire too, but the Davis boys were already at it. Teeth chattering, they put some kindling in the airtight heater, poured a little kerosene on it, and lit it. In a few moments, the crackling flames were beginning to chase away the grinding cold of the cabin.

Barney stood for a brief instant beside the stove, letting the heat thaw the arthritis from his stiffening fingers. When he spoke a few moments before, his voice had been calm and undisturbed, but there was an unmistakable sag to his shoulders and concern gleamed in his eyes.

Del turned to him. "Where do you suppose he's gone?"

"Maybe he went out to work his traps," Doug broke in.

"In the dark?"

Barney left the stove and went over to the corner of the cabin where they had stacked their gear.

"The big flashlight is gone," he said. "You must be right, Doug. He must've gone out to work his traps."

"But why would he do that, when we're here to help him? It doesn't make sense!"

* * *

When George Aubichon had gone to bed that night, he hadn't planned on leaving the cabin without the others. But, in spite of the fact that he was exhausted, sleep would not come. Every time he closed his eyes, he would see his grandfather's serious face and hear his kindly voice reading from the Bible.

He didn't know why Doug and Del had to agree with his grandfather and talk about Jesus Christ. It wouldn't be so bad if he had the boys to stand with him; then he wouldn't feel so alone.

George began to blame his grandfather for it. The old man wouldn't let him alone; he had to keep preaching at him all the time.

If only those words hadn't driven to the very depths of his heart. They stung so deeply, he couldn't think of anything else. It was no wonder he couldn't sleep.

George didn't know exactly how he came to decide to go out and work his traps alone so early in the morning, before anyone else was up. He didn't know quite how he figured that would repay his grandfather for trying to talk to him so much about his need for giving his heart to Christ. But, somehow, he reached the point where he felt that he had to get that wolverine on his own, in order to prove himself to his grandfather and to Del and Doug.

Let them think he was so stupid he had to have help to catch the raider who had been stealing from his traps. He'd show them. They'd find out he wasn't quite as ignorant as they thought he was.

He would take his .22 rifle and go out and hide at one of the sets. Then, when the wolverine came along, he'd shine the light on him and shoot him. When he came back with the animal who had been causing all the trouble, his grandfather would have to admit George didn't need the help Barney seemed to think he needed. And Del and Doug would find out what kind of a woodsman and trapper he really was. It would make up for all of the aching they had caused in George's heart.

Quietly the boy got out of bed, dressed, and found the flashlight his grandfather brought along. With that, he slipped out into the frigid night air.

It didn't take long for George to go to the first trap. Cautiously he shined his light on it. The wolverine hadn't been there yet. He was in luck! He would go over to that little clump of brush and— His foot slipped, and he sprawled forward. The force of his fall sent his gun scooting across the snow. He threw out his hand in a desperate attempt to catch it.

There was a harsh, metallic snap. Pain shot up his arm in great, driving waves. He was caught in the trap!

9

Midwinter Nightmare

BARNEY MADE BREAKFAST and calmly sat down at the table with Del and Doug. He seemed to be as unhurried and deliberate as though his grandson, George, was there with them. Only when they bowed their heads to ask God's blessing on the food, did he reveal his concern. He prayed, asking God to take care of George and to keep him safe from harm.

"And, our Father," he went on quietly, "help George to turn his life over to You completely. Help him to listen to You and to walk the way You want him to walk." His tone revealed that, in spite of his outward calm, the elderly Indian was most disturbed by his grandson's disappearance.

When he finished praying, they sat at the table uneasily, trying to keep from showing each other the depth of their concern.

At last Del could control himself no longer. He turned to his Indian friend. "Where do you suppose he went, Barney?"

The portly Cree slowly set his cup of coffee back on the table. It was some time before he spoke. "I don't know for sure," he said, "but thinking back on it, I've got a hunch he probably cooked up some scheme to try to catch the wolverine on his own."

"He already found out he couldn't do that," Del said.

"He was discouraged, all right, but he didn't much like the idea of my coming along." The old man sighed deeply. "I could have let him quit trapping or come back here alone. Maybe that's what I should've done. But I didn't figure he'd be able to get the wolverine without help."

Del nodded. He didn't know anything about trapping wolverines, himself; he had never even seen one. But he did know enough about the wild animals of the North to appreciate the knowledge of someone like Barney, who had spent so much of his life on a trapline. If he had been in George's place, he'd have been glad for the chance to find out how an expert would go about trapping.

After breakfast they had another time of Bible-reading and prayer. Then they sat back and waited for the coming of daylight.

Shortly after dawn, Barney lumbered over to the

place where they had hung their coats and took down his parka. The boys watched him as he put it on and pulled on his mukluks and rubbers.

"What are you going to do now?" Doug asked. He didn't like the idea of Barney going out in the sharp, subzero wind, and his face reflected his agitation.

The Indian spoke simply. "I'm going out to find George."

Both boys jumped up quickly. "We'd better go along."

"There's no need of that."

"But you might need help."

Barney Aubichon hesitated. He glanced in the direction of the window, as though noting the cold and the bitter, wind-swirled snow. "You'd better stay here," he told them. "George may be real cold when I find him. The cabin should be warm when we get back." He paused momentarily. "Besides, there's a possibility that George might come back while we're gone. If he doesn't find us here, there's no telling what he's apt to do. He might go out to look for us, and that would only make things worse."

Del's lips narrowed thoughtfully. He wasn't quite sure whether Barney was giving them a real reason for staying behind, or whether this was an excuse, because he was afraid to have them out in such a driving storm. But, whatever it was, the old Indian's mind was not to be changed; Del could tell by the way he spoke. Barney had decided that this was the way the matter should be handled. As far as he was concerned, that settled it.

Before leaving the warmth of the cabin to go out and look for his grandson, Barney turned back to Del and Doug once more. "I want you to chop some more wood, boys, and pile it inside."

"That'll only take a few minutes," Doug protested.

"It'll take longer than that to get the amount of wood we'll be needing if this storm keeps on."

The boys nodded in agreement. "We'll take care of it."

"And another thing. When that's done, I don't want you to start thinking you ought to come out and look for me. I want you both to promise me that you'll stay in the cabin."

"But—"

"If you do come out to look for George and me, we'll have a bigger problem on our hands than we've got now."

Del protested that they had been around the woods long enough to go where they wanted to without getting lost. "You don't have to worry about us. We can take care of ourselves."

"Maybe you can, but I want you to promise me that you'll stay here, just the same."

The boys gave him their word, when they realized he wouldn't leave until they did.

"We'll stay here," Del told him. "We'll promise you that."

"Fine." He turned and opened the door. "If you want to help, pray for us." With that, he stepped out into the icy blast.

Del and Doug stood at the window uneasily and watched him go. They were even more upset than they had been before, as Barney slogged up the path on his snowshoes and disappeared from view.

"I sure wish old Barney would have let us go with him," Del said after a time. "He's not well enough to go traipsing around in the bush on snowshoes."

"You can say that again."

"He wouldn't even have come out here if he hadn't wanted to help George."

"That guy! Somebody ought to kick him for pulling a trick like this!' '

"And when Barney finds him, he'll probably laugh his head off because we were so worried about him."

*   *   *

Out on the trapline, George Aubichon writhed miserably in the snow, pain slamming through his young body in great sledgehammer blows. At first, as he felt the bite of the trap on his arm, he cried out in terror; but now reason took hold of him. It was useless for him to scream for help. There was no one within two miles to come and help him get his wrist and hand out of the savage trap.

For the space of several minutes, he lay quite still, conserving his strength and trying to figure out what to do next. He just might be able to get out of the trap, if he could stand so he could press down on the spring with his foot.

He looked at the trap once more and hope fled. It had a double spring, one on each side. He would have to press both of them down at the same time to free himself. He had been working with traps enough the past years to know that such a task was not simple. He lay motionless in the snow, panting heavily.

George was well aware of the seriousness of his position. He had left the trapping cabin without telling anyone where he was going. They didn't even know when he left. It might be hours before he was even missed.

And already the cold was biting through his parka and mukluks, driving to the marrow of his bones. It was a searing, numbing cold that pressed with relentless power against his consciousness, clamping itself on his lithe body, and dulling his mind until he all but lost his capacity to think.

If he just hadn't been so upset with his grandfather for trying to talk with him about Jesus Christ and the Bible and his need for a Saviour, he wouldn't be in a mess like this. What had happened was his own fault. He realized that now. But it didn't do any good to think about that. It wasn't going to help him any.

As he lay there, fighting pain, George began to defend himself. *In a way it wasn't my fault,* he reasoned. *Anybody would be apt to get so upset he'd do something stupid if somebody was preaching at him all the time.* He couldn't help it that he thought he had to get away from his grandfather.

When it came right down to it, it was the old man's fault. He was the one who had caused all the trouble. And the worst of it was that George was the one who was having to suffer for it.

The boy's temper raged as he struggled to his feet, grimacing against the pain that surged through his body; and he tried to open the trap. He battled grimly, but he was in such an awkward position he was even unable to ease the pressure on the jaws of the trap, let alone to free himself.

A sob jerked from between his lips as he collapsed on the snow. He lay there motionless, swallowed in the agony that had taken hold of him.

This wasn't real. It couldn't be. No trapper got himself caught in his own trap! It just didn't happen. It was all a bitter, ugly dream, brought on by his grandfather's preaching. He closed his eyes momentarily, as though he was actually back in the warm cabin, dreaming that this terrible thing was happening. But the steadily increasing cold and the excruciating pain told him well enough that it was all too true. He *had* been caught in his own trap! And, as if that weren't enough, he would soon freeze to death, unless he was able to free himself.

George pulled himself to a sitting position and looked about, frantically. If he could only manage to work the stake free, he could make it back to the cabin somehow, and Del and Doug and his grandfather would be able to get his hand out of the trap. He crawled over to the place where Barney had driven the stake into a green tree. But, even as he forced his fingers to close around it, he realized that it would be impossible for him to pull the stake out. His grandfather had driven it down to the chain. With an ax or a hatchet and a good right hand, he could probably work it free. As it was, it was useless for him even to try.

George sank once more to the snow, his own terror climbing. It's snowing harder, he noted. In a few minutes he could be caught in a blinding blizzard. If that happened, nobody would be able to find him. He was done! Finished! In desperation, he closed his eyes and tried to pray.

He had heard other people pray often enough around home. But how could *he* talk to God? he wondered miserably. What made him think God would listen to him? George drifted fitfully to unconsciousness.

How long he lay there, he didn't know. It may have been a few moments. It may have been an hour or more. All he was sure about was that the pain did not relax. It kept driving in, blow upon blow. Nausea caught him in the pit of his stomache and, once or twice, as he came to, he thought he was going to vomit. But he was soon unconscious again and didn't even hear Barney come stumbling over the trail, until he cried out in alarm.

"George!" His grandfather shouted, his voice breaking fearfully.

The boy stirred and opened his eyes as his grandfather floundered through the drifts and knelt beside him.

"George!" he cried loudly. "You're hurt!"

The boy stiffened at the sound of his grandfather's voice and opened his eyes. For a brief heartbeat he had to fight to keep from crying.

"You're caught in the trap! I was afraid of something like this!"

Barney's breathing was labored as he loosed the

powerful jaws of the trap, and his grandson managed to free his hand. Once his arm was out of the viselike grip, the boy reeled. At first it hadn't seemed possible that he had been caught. Now it didn't seem possible that he had been freed. He moistened his lips and looked up at his grandfather.

The old man's eyes were glazed, and his face was strangely white.

"Grandpa!" George cried. "What's the matter? What's wrong?"

Before Barney could reply, his knees buckled, and he collapsed in the snow.

10

Snowy Rescue

FRANTICALLY, George Aubichon bent over his grandfather who was lying prone and motionless in the snow. The boy's dark eyes were wide with fear, and his breath came out betwen his teeth in long, tearing gasps. His own pain was forgotten for the moment. Something terrible had happened; he didn't know what!

"Grandpa!" he shouted against the howling wind. "Grandpa! What's the matter?"

At the sound of the boy's voice, Barney stirred and groaned feebly. A new agony clenched his teeth and held his body rigid. Something seemed to pinch against his chest until he could not move, and his breathing was shallow and labored.

"What *is* it?" George cried. "What happened, Grandpa?"

Barney's lips parted, and he struggled to speak; but no sound escaped his lips.

George thought no more about the hurt in his own wrist and arm where the trap had clamped so viciously on him. He hadn't been around his grandfather Aubichon very much for the last two years, but he had often heard his mother and dad talking about Grandpa's bad heart.

Now this had happened! And it was all his fault! A dry, aching sob choked in his throat. If something bad happened to his grandpa, George didn't think he could stand it!

Barney's eyes opened slightly, and he looked around. The boy bent closer. "Grandpa!"

"George!" His voice was trembling and little more than a whisper. "George!"

The boy bent closer until his ear was almost at his grandfather's mouth. "What is it? Are—are you all right, Grandpa?"

The old man hesitated, and it was all he could do to talk. "I—I don't think I can get up and walk, George." The effort of speaking was enough to bring temporary exhaustion. He closed his eyes momentarily, and he pulled in his breath in quick gasps.

George studied his grandfather's ashen face uneasily, his fear continuing to grow. Grandpa had always been so big and so strong, the sort of man who could walk farther and carry bigger loads and do more work than anyone else. George had never thought that he would ever be sick, that anything could ever cause him to quit. Now he was lying helpless in the snow.

The boy pulled in a tortured breath and expelled the air with a rush. "I can't go, Grandpa!" he exclaimed. "I can't leave you!"

"But you have to!" The old man's voice sounded desperate.

Reluctantly, George raised up and backed away. "I—I'll be back out here just as quick as I can."

Barney Aubichon nodded and closed his eyes, trying to stop the searing pain.

George ran across the rough terrain, stumbling now and again in his haste. Once he sprawled in the snow. A few moments later, he caught a snowshoe on a fallen log and sprawled against a tree.

* * *

Time dragged by as Del and Doug Davis waited in the little cabin for Barney to come back with his grandson. They had eaten breakfast and washed the dishes and cut all the wood they could possibly need. At the moment they were sitting close to the airtight heater, soaking up the warmth, and trying to ignore their feelings of uneasiness.

For the seventh time, Doug turned to his brother. "What time is it, Del?" he asked.

The other boy glanced nervously at his watch.

"It's only ten minutes later than it was the last time you asked me."

Doug ignored his remark. "I sure thought Barney would have found George and come back here by this time."

"You don't suppose he went on back to the village, do you?"

"He wouldn't do that."

"I didn't think he'd do a lot of things," Del retorted.

Doug rose and put another stick of wood on the fire. "I guess you've got something there. But I can't help thinking about something else. You—you don't suppose something has happened to one of them, do you?"

Del did not voice his own growing concern. He got to his feet, stood for a moment in front of the chair, and walked uneasily across the rough pine floor to peer out the one clear corner of the frost-rimmed window.

"I don't like this," Del said. "They should have been back here a long time ago."

Doug nodded. "Maybe we ought to go out and look for them."

"We can't do that," his brother said quickly. "We gave Barney our word that we wouldn't leave the cabin. We told him we'd stay here, no matter what happened. We can't go back on that."

"We can't leave them out there. We've got to go out and see what's happened to them. If we don't, there's no knowing what'll happen to them."

They were still discussing the matter, when there was a sound outside the door.

"Doug!" George cried in desperation. "Del! Come quick!"

"They're out here now!" Doug cried.

At the sound of the Indian boy's vioce, both Del and Doug ran to the door and flung it open. George was floundering through the snow, terror twisting his young face.

"George!" Del cried.

He stopped a few feet from the cabin door, straddle-legged, his injured arm hanging grotesquely at his side. For one brief instant they stared at him before Doug ran out to him.

"What is it? What's wrong?"

"Come quick!" he shouted. His voice broke, and he acted as though he was about to whirl and dash back into the bush.

"What's happened?" Doug repeated, tautly.

"It's Grandpa!" The boy kicked off his snow-shoes and burst into the cabin, his eyes wide and staring.

The Davis boys followed him, pressing their questions on him. "What's happened to him? Is he hurt? Where is he?"

"I—I don't know whether he's had a heart attack or what's wrong!" He was so upset he was almost incoherent. "But he's lying out there in the bush! He—he couldn't even get up!" The words choked in his throat. "You've got to come quick and help him!"

The Davis boys struggled into their heavy parkas and boots, frantically. "Where is he?"

"Out at the first beaver set." He hurried to the door once more and rushed outside. "Hurry!"

George tied his snowshoes in place and would have slogged away but Doug stopped him.

"Now, wait a minute. Let's figure out exactly what we're going to do, before we go charging off."

"But we've got to get him back here, or to the village, or something ! If we don't, he'll die!"

"We can't carry him," Del said, "that's for sure."

"I hadn't thought of that."

The corners of Del's mouth tightened thoughtfully. "We've got the toboggan here. We can take that and put him on it. Then if we should have to move him back to the village, we'll have a way of doing it."

"That's a good idea," Doug agreed. "We'd need it, anyway, to bring him back here."

Doug grabbed the toboggan rope, as they pushed hurriedly through the deep snow, pulling it behind him. In spite of the fact that he had run all the way back to the cabin and had turned around without rest, and was going back, George Aubichon was still several paces ahead.

The boys prayed inwardly as they went, asking God to be with their old Indian friend who was lying helpless at one of the traps. Grimly, Doug and Del ignored the cold and the fitful snow squalls and the wind. Regardless of what happened, they had to get to Barney and fast! He couldn't survive long in such cold! That was all the determination they needed to get out to the beaver set as quickly as possible.

As the boys caught up to George, doggedly plodding through the drifting snow, George told them what had taken place since he sneaked out of the cabin before daylight that morning.

"Why did you leave, anyway?" Del demanded. "We were all going to go out with you to work your traps this morning. You didn't have to go alone."

George looked away from them. "I—I know that, but I decided I—I wanted to get the wolverine alone, if I could. I didn't want to have help!"

Doug started to reply that the Indian boy had made a stupid decision, but he checked himself. George already felt badly enough about what had happened; there was no point in making him feel any worse.

"Maybe you should've stayed back in the cabin," Del said when he told about getting his arm caught in the trap.

"I couldn't do that!" he retorted quickly. "I had to come along and—and help with Grandpa!"

"We could manage."

"It didn't hurt me very bad," George continued. "I had my heavy parka on, and about the only thing that happened to me was that I couldn't get out of the trap by myself."

"Then how—?"

"Grandpa came and was so excited when he saw that I was caught in the trap, that—" His voice choked and it was a moment or two before he could continue. "He worked so fast to get me free, that I—I think maybe it caused him to have a—a heart attack." George stopped abruptly. "If something terrible happens to him because of this, it'll be all my fault."

Del Davis spoke up, roughly. "You can't talk that way," he ordered. "You can't even think that way."

"But it's true!"

"Maybe it is," Doug broke in, "but we can't worry about that now. We've got to find him and get him back to the village as quickly as we can, so your folks'll be able to help him!"

Fighting the storm and the drifts, sapped the

strength from the boys' legs and snatched the breath from their nostrils. Every now and again they had to pause to rest, hunching their backs against the fury of the wind. Del wondered if George knew where he was going, but he plunged onward without hesitation: and at last, they reached the place where Barney was lying, his huge figure half covered by new snow.

"There he is!" George shouted, bursting into a staggering run. "Grandpa! Grandpa!"

Del and Doug plunged forward anxiously until they reached his side. For an instant or more after they reached him the elderly Indian lay motionless. Fear caught in Del's heart. Were they too late after all?

"Barney!" Doug cried, kneeling beside him. "Barney! it's us! We've come back after you!"

The old man stirred slightly, and his eyes fluttered. He did not move anymore, but at least they know that he was still alive. They breathed a prayer of thanksgiving.

"Grandpa!" George exclaimed, almost shouting against the howling wind.

Barney opened his eyes once more, and a faint smile rested briefly on his lips. "Thank God you came!" he murmured between pain-clenched teeth. "Thank God you came!" The simple statement was a prayer.

Doug and Del glanced at each other, concern gleaming in their eyes; but when they spoke, they tried to sound calm and confident that everything would work out all right.

"We'll help lift you onto the toboggan, Barney," Doug said, "and have you back to the village in no time."

"That's right. And you're not even going to have to walk. We'll pull you all the way."

"That's not going to be as easy as you think it is," Barney whispered.

"Don't you worry about that. We'll make it there, all right."

The boys had Barney on the toboggan in a moment or two and tucked the heavy blankets around him.

"How do you feel now, Grandpa?" George wanted to know.

"I—I think maybe I don't have quite as much pain now as I had at first."

"Well," Doug said, "let's get with it. We've got quite a ways to go!"

With that, they started back to the village, two of them pulling the toboggan, the third staying behind. It was all they could do to keep it moving in the heavy snow.

11

A Prayer Answered by Air

BACK IN THE ISOLATED Saskatchewan village, George Aubichon's stepmother was home alone. She had just been down to the lake to fill the water buckets, against the possibility that they were in for a blizzard, and brought in the last of the wood her husband had cut before leaving that morning. She saw the boys trudging through the snow toward the house, when they were still some distance away. At first she thought nothing about it, except that the boys were coming back sooner than she thought they would; but as they drew closer, she realized that her husband's father was not walking with them.

And then she saw the big bulk on the toboggan! Something had happened! Something terrible!

"George!" Her voice shrilled on the still winter air, echoing across the village and to the fishermen

halfway across the lake. "George, what happened?"
She dashed forward hurriedly.

"It's Grandpa!" he gasped, the words tumbling
out in anguish. "He's awful sick!"

"What happened?" she repeated.

"We think he had a heart attack or something."

Barney opened his eyes, feebly. "I—I'll be all
right. I just ran out of gas out there," he said, trying to be funny.

Mrs. Aubichon took charge of the situation calmly. "Let's get him into the house and on the bed."

Barney raised himself on one elbow, with effort.
"You don't have to carry me. I can walk."

"Maybe you can," his daughter-in-law said quietly, "but I think it would be better if you'd let us
help you, OK?"

He tried to struggle to his feet, but settled back
on the toboggan, breathing heavily. "I suppose
you're right, at that. I didn't know I was so weak."

"We'll help you," Del put in.

The four of them managed to get the portly old
Indian off of the toboggan and into the house and
into bed. Even with the help of the boys and his
son's wife, the exertion was enough to cause Barney's hands and shoulders to tremble convulsively.

Once they had him in bed, Mrs. Aubichon went
into another room to get an extra blanket for him.
George followed her, closing the door behind them.

"Mom," he said in a coarse whisper.

She turned to face him. "Yes?"

"Is Grandpa going to be all right?" Tension softened his voice.

His mother did not reply immediately.

"He *is* going to be all right, isn't he?"

For the first time, her lips trembled. "We'll have to pray that he is," she answered nervously.

The last traces of color fled from the boy's cheeks, and his shoulders quivered. "I—I didn't mean to cause any trouble," he murmured defensively. "I—I—"

"I'm sure you didn't."

George eyed her questioningly. That was a switch, he told himself. She hadn't been understanding before. At least, that was the way he preferred to think about her. Everybody said that stepmothers were mean and cold and unforgiving. It bothered him a little to see that she was being gentle and kind.

A strange thought crept in at the corners of his mind. Maybe the trouble was with *him*. Maybe she had been sympathetic all along, and he had pretended she was just the opposite.

"What can we do for Grandpa?" he continued, nervously.

She shook her head. "There's really not much that we can do, except to keep him quiet, and pray that Mr. Orlis will come back with the plane so he can take him to a doctor."

The boy wiped an unsteady hand across his face. If something happened to his grandfather, he thought he would never get over it.

In the bedroom, Del and Doug were alone with their old friend. His breathing was so shallow they could scarcely tell whether he was breathing at all. They didn't know anything about medicine, but they knew that Barney was awfully sick.

Del left his place beside the bed and moved to the window where he looked out at the slate gray sky.

If only Danny would get back!

The hours dragged endlessly. Barney lay motionless in the bedroom of the little Saskatchewan cabin. His face was pale and drawn, against the white sheets, and his eyes were tightly closed. Only by watching him closely was it possible to tell that he was still breathing.

His daughter-in-law hovered over him, and from time to time, Del and Doug Davis tiptoed into the bedroom with George to look silently down at their elderly Indian friend. Occasionally his muscles twitched, and a thin groan of pain escaped his lips. Most of the time, however, he lay still, as though he lacked the strength to move.

Although George's stepmother held her emotions

severely in check, it was obvious that her concern for the sick man was growing. Every few minutes she took his pulse, frowning as she did so. She didn't mention how high it was, or that it was weak and fluttering; but the way she shuffled about the room and kept coming back to the bed, revealed her deepest fears.

Del, who had taken up a vigil at the head of Barney's bed for the past few minutes, glanced up at Doug, his eyes whispering uneasiness that he dare not voice.

George was equally upset. He followed his mother out of the bedroom and talked to her in guarded tones.

"He's awful sick, isn't he?"

She nodded without speaking.

"Do—do you think he'll die?"

"We shouldn't talk about that, George!" she exclaimed sternly. "We shouldn't even *think* such a thing!"

"Isn't there anything we can do, Mom?"

She frowned in reply. "There isn't anything that anybody can do for him now," she said, "unless we can get him to a doctor!"

"We could do that!" the boy retorted excitedly. "I could borrow some dogs or a power toboggan! We could start out now and have him at the hospital before dark!"

She turned to the window and looked out at the lowering sky. "I've been thinking about that, but I don't think he would be able to stand the trip. He's *awful* sick!"

While they were talking, Doug motioned Del toward the bedroom door with a significant jerk of his head.

"Come outside for a minute," he murmured.

He didn't think Barney would hear him, but he did. The old man opened his eyes and managed a weak smile. "Don't you boys worry about me. I'll be all right."

"Sure you will." Del reached down and touched Barney's pudgy hand with his own trembling fingers.

"All I need is a little rest, and I'll be as good as new."

Mrs. Aubichon and the boys left the bedroom a moment later and closed the door against their voices.

"The only one I know who could possibly get Grandpa to the doctor safely and in time to help him is Danny Orlis." Mrs. Aubichon turned to the Davis boys. "When do you think he'll be back?"

The boys eyed each other questioningly. "I don't know for sure," Del replied. "I thought he'd be back here long before this, didn't you?"

"I sure did, but you never can tell. He could

have had some extra flying to do somewhere, or he could have had engine trouble, or maybe the weather where he is just wasn't fit for flying. It doesn't take a lot to cause delays this time of the year."

George's mother ran her hand nervously across her dark face. "We've got to do something to get help for him as soon as possible. Maybe we ought to have someone radio for a plane. They could probably have the air ambulance in here by tomorrow morning."

"We'll do that for you, Mrs. Aubichon," Doug put in quickly.

"Thank you. You boys have been such a help to us."

As they went to get their parkas, a faint groan drifted in from the bedroom. Del started. "That's Barney!" he exclaimed.

"Do you suppose he's getting worse?" George demanded fearfully.

Instantly his stepmother started for the bedroom. "Whatever you do, tell am to hurry! Tell them it's an emergency! We've got to have the air ambulance here as soon as possible."

The three boys left the cabin, half running through the snow in the direction of the Hudson Bay store. Two or three men on the path stared at the boys as they hurried by.

"I sure thought Danny would be back here before this," Del said as they ran. "When he left, he talked as though he would only be gone for a few days."

Doug started to reply, but stopped suddenly. "Listen!"

They all came to a halt, staring at one another.

"What is it?" George wanted to know.

For several seconds, Doug did not answer him. Instead, he cocked his head to one side, listening attentively.

"What is it?" George demanded a second time, insistently.

The sound was getting louder now. It gathered strength and body as the moments passed, until there was no longer any doubt about it.

"It's a plane!" Del cried.

George Aubichon's eyes widened, and he stared up at the gray sky. He had heard that sound often enough himself, but now it scarcely seemed possible that it could be an aircraft.

"Are you sure?" he asked uncertainly.

"Don't you hear it?"

By this time, even George had to admit there was no mistaking the dull, insistent drone. The sound of the engine was growing louder with each passing moment.

"You're right!" Awe crept into the Indian boy's voice. "It is a plane!"

The boys spun to face the direction the sound was coming from. At first they could only hear the approaching aircraft; but in an instant, a faint pink speck appeared against the distant sky. George Aubichon cried out with glee, his shout echoing and reechoing on the still, cold air.

"That's him!" he shouted. "That's him!"

"Thank God!" Del breathed prayerfully. "He answered our prayers!"

Mrs. Aubichon had heard the sound of the aircraft, too. The cabin door popped open, and she dashed out to stare up at the clouds.

Danny Orlis was back!

That was all any of them could think about! Danny would soon be on the ground.

"Do you think he'll leave with Grandpa tonight?" George asked hopefully, as he and the Davis boys ran down to the lake where the plane would be landing.

"I don't know about that," Doug said. It was already quite late in the afternoon. He rather thought that Danny would leave immediately for the nearest hospital with him, but he couldn't be sure. There was one thing certain. Danny Orlis wouldn't be taking any chances. Unless he was sure he could get to the place where he was going before dark, he wouldn't take off.

12

One Problem Solved

WHEN DANNY LANDED, Del, Doug, and George were there to meet him.

"Well, are your bags packed?" he asked. "We have to get cracking if we want to be out of here in time to make it to Saskatoon before dark."

"Something terrible has happened," Del told him. "Barney's awful sick."

Concern leaped to the pilot's eyes. "That's too bad. What happened?"

Hurriedly they told him. Danny turned quickly to George. "What does your mother say she thinks is wrong with him?"

The boy shrugged. "She says she doesn't really know anything for sure, but she thinks it's a heart attack. I guess his pulse is real fast and sort of funny. One time it's strong, and the next time it's so faint she can hardly find it. Mom keeps saying she

119

hopes you'll get here soon so you could take him to Saskatoon to a hospital."

Danny directed his attention to the Davis boys.

"Del, I'd like to have you go back to the cabin with George and tell his mother to get ready to leave with Barney right away. And you, Doug, help me refuel."

Del whirled and dashed away, with George following close behind.

By the time Danny Orlis and Doug had the aircraft filled with gas and the engine idling, Del, George, and Mrs. Aubichon had put Barney on the toboggan, wrapped heavily in blankets, and pulled him down to the plane.

"Oh, I'm so thankful you're here!" Mrs. Aubichon exclaimed. "You're an answer to prayer."

"We can thank God for that," Danny told her. "Come on, you guys. Give me a hand with Barney."

"Is there room for me to go along?" Mrs. Aubichon asked.

Danny nodded. "I figured you'd like to go with us."

They had already taken out one of the seats and soon had Barney loaded into the plane. The old Indian's daughter-in-law got in beside him. The boys watched tensely as Danny taxied to the far end of the landing strip, turned, and allowed the engine to idle for a few moments before roaring down the lake to take off.

George glanced nervously at Del and Doug. "Do—do you think he'll get Grandpa to the hospital in time?" he asked.

Del spoke softly. "We'll have to pray that he does."

The three boys lingered along the lakeshore until the aircraft disappeared from view.

"You know," George said at last, "this is all my fault. Grandpa wouldn't have gotten sick if I hadn't done such a stupid trick as sneaking off in the early morning alone."

Doug answered, "What you did wasn't the smartest thing in the world, that's for sure, but we don't know that you caused Barney to be sick."

"Sure we do. If I hadn't been such a know-it-all, I wouldn't have sneaked out of the cabin and got myself caught in the trap. And if that hadn't happened, Grandpa wouldn't have had to come after me." He pulled in a deep breath. "I don't care what you say. I know that I'm the one who caused him to have his heart attack." The words lodged in his throat. "And if something happens to him, it'll be my fault."

They walked thoughtfully back to the cabin together. There was little they could think of except

Barney and the plane and the hospital Danny hoped to get him to.

"I don't know why I do the dumb things I do," George continued. "I never do anything right."

"Nobody's perfect," Del told him. "It's just natural for us to do things we shouldn't. The Bible tells us we're that way because of the sin in our lives."

George eyed him narrowly, a sullen anger clouding his face. "All I need right now is for you to preach at me. That's going to make me feel real good."

"I'm not going to preach at you. I was just explaining that the Bible says nobody is righteous. It tells us that none of us live the way God says we should live. So, you do things you shouldn't do, and so do we."

Doug spoke up. "That's the reason we have such a hard time doing the things that are right. It isn't natural for us to do things that are good."

George went over and sat down near the table.

"You guys are sure a lot of help." Sarcasm honed his voice.

"But the thing you've got to remember is that you don't have to stay the way you are. Del and I didn't have to, and neither do you."

"What do you mean by that?" He really didn't want to ask the question. It just popped out.

"We can be different if we want to," Doug con-

tinued. "We can confess our sin and put our trust
in the Lord Jesus Christ to save us from the kind of
lives we have been leading and to make new persons
of us."

George thought about that. He had heard the
same kind of talk from his grandfather ever since he
could remember.

"Well, I—I know I need to become a Christian,
and I'll probably do it someday, but right now I'm
too worried about my grandfather to do anything
else."

Doug and Del didn't want to accept that as an
answer. "That's all the more reason you ought to
put your trust in Jesus Christ. Your grandfather
would tell you the same thing, if he were here."

The Indian boy was quiet and thoughtful for a
long while. Finally he spoke. "Not now."

Doug wasn't satisfied. "George, God loved you so
much that He sent Jesus to die on the cross so you
could have your sins forgiven and go to heaven."

It was two or three minutes before George spoke
again.

"I told you that I'd do it some time," the Indian
boy retorted irritably, "but not now."

"But George—"

"I said, 'not now!'" With that he stormed into
his bedroom and slammed the door, leaving Del
and Doug alone, staring at each other.

The Davis boys and George Aubichon expected Danny Orlis to radio the Hudson Bay store in the village as soon as they took Barney to the Saskatoon hospital. However, it was not until noon the following day that they heard from the missionary pilot.

An Indian boy about their age came to the Aubichon house with a message from Danny.

"Here's a telegram about your grandpa, George," the boy said, handing the folded sheet of paper to his friend.

George took it fearfully. "Is—is he all right?"

The messenger did not reply.

George ripped open the folded sheet of paper and read it aloud. "Grandpa in hospital doing fine." There was more, but the Indian lad's voice choked as he realized that his grandfather was going to live.

Del and Doug breathed a silent prayer of thanksgiving.

"That's great!" Del exclaimed.

"Wait a minute. There's more. 'Del and Doug be ready to leave when I get back.' "

George Aubichon's smile fled. "I sure don't want to see you guys go."

"We don't want to go either," Doug told him, "but we have to get back to Fairview and go to school. We've already missed a few days now."

For a minute or two, the boys debated whether

Danny would be coming back that day or not. Finally they decided that they would have to be ready to go, just to be on the safe side.

"It wouldn't hurt for you to stay just one more night," George said.

"Maybe not, but Danny's not going to feel that way. When he says we should be ready to leave, he wants us to be ready. He'll be on our necks, if we're not."

George saw that he could not convince them to wait about packing, so he went into the bedroom and sat on the edge of the bed while they packed their gear.

"I'm sure glad you guys came." He breathed deeply. "It's really been great to have you here."

The Davis boys both looked up. "We've enjoyed it, too. And we're sure sorry about your grandfather. But we'll be praying for him. And for you, too."

George's face clouded, and he looked as though the tears might rush to his eyes. "Thanks. And I meant what I said. Someday I will become a Christian. But not right now."

Del wanted to say more to him about it, but there was no chance to do so. George had already closed his mind.

Del and Doug hadn't been sure when Danny would come back, but an hour after they finished packing, he flew in. He talked briefly with George and a couple of friends of the Aubichon family, explaining what the doctor had done and how Barney was getting along.

"Apparently he's going to be fine," the missionary pilot said. "The doctor took some extensive tests last night and this morning and decided that he still had time to control his condition. Barring some unexpected trouble, he seemed to think Barney ought to be OK."

Relief gleamed in George's eyes.

"Your mother is going to be staying in Saskatoon for a few days, George," Danny went on, "so she said you should stay with her sister."

The boy nodded.

"Your grandfather'll have to stay in the hospital for a while; but when he's able to leave, I'll come up and take him back to Minnesota."

Del and Doug were in the aircraft and Danny was about to join them, when he paused and turned back to the Indian boy.

"Oh, yes, I almost forgot. What did you decide about school? Your grandfather wanted me to find out."

George's grin flashed.

"Tell him I've changed my mind since I've been around Doug and Del. If they feel like they need to go to school, I want to go too."

Danny nodded and put out his hand to George. "Good. I'll pass that word on to him."

Feeling very relieved, Del thought of another question. "Then what about the wolverine?"

George grinned. "I want to do a good job in school now, so I won't have time for trapping. Besides," he added sheepishly, "I know when I'm licked."

A few minutes later in the aircraft heading back toward Saskatoon and Fairview, Danny turned to the Davis boys. "Well, you had some effect on George while you were here. At least he's going to stay in school."

"If we could only have made him see his need for turning his life over to Jesus Christ," Doug said. "Then I'd feel as though we had really accomplished something."

"He did listen when we talked to him," Del added, "and he said he wanted to become a Christian someday."

"Someday!" Doug's voice was sorrowful. "Maybe he won't have another chance!"

Danny Orlis nodded. Salvation was one thing that shouldn't be put off. No one can know how much time he has left in this life. Some people might have plenty of time, but others don't.

"It would have been much safer for George if he'd decided now," he said.

As the plane headed southward, the boys' hearts were sad. They hated to have to leave Barney in a hospital so far away, and they hated to leave George with his spiritual future unsettled.

Staring out at the clouds, Del took slight comfort from George's promise that he would give himself to Christ, "someday." Del whispered, "Make it someday *soon*, George."